Prodigy
Soul of the Witch Saga - Book 1
C. Marie Bowen

Pixler Publications

Prodigy

Soul of the Witch Saga – Book 1

by C. Marie Bowen

This book was previously published as *Coven Moon, Book 1*.

ISBN-13: 978-1-9425-186 – Paperback

ISBN-13: 978-1-9425-179 – EPUB

Cover Design by C. Marie Bowen

Published by Pixler Publications

Discover other titles by C. Marie Bowen at www.cmariebowen.com

Contents

Chapter 1

Ayden MacKenna

—

Late July 1841 – Northern Connecticut

Flames danced across the blackened firewood. The logs were scorched white along the top, and one end had already fallen to ash. Its slow hypnotic undulation drew Ayden in, spoke to him with vague images like half-remembered dreams. He lay curled on his side beneath one of the family's two wagons. His eyelids grew heavy as he listened to his parents talk beside the fire.

They'd come a long way today and would have another long ride tomorrow. The wagons held everything the small family possessed. Moving from New Haven to Boston was not Ayden's choice, but he didn't have a voice in such matters at thirteen years old.

While strange figures acted out their silent pantomime inside the fire, Ayden thought about the friends he'd left behind. He'd played with the younger children from his parents' coven each month, but he'd never had a best friend, not really.

"Tell me what Leader Franklin said again," his mother murmured as she stirred the wooden embers with a long stick. She looked up and smiled at Ayden's father.

"Franklin said his cousin owns a farm this side of Boston and leads a small local coven. Mr. Franklin believes this cousin, a Mr. Garrett Brown, may be willing to put in a good word in town for me and help us get back on our feet." Weariness laced his father's voice. He rested his arm on his thigh as he spoke into the fire. "We're due for some good luck, and this could be it. There may be a farrier position in Boston, and a word up from a local man would give me a better chance." He shook his head. "I love you, Rachael, and I promise to make this up to you."

"You've nothing to make up, Lyam, my love." She placed her hand over her husband's arm. "You've given me everything. Losing your position to someone willing to do your job for less—" She shrugged and shook her head. "Your employer doesn't realize their mistake in letting you go, but they will." Their words blended into the sounds of the night while the waxing gibbous moon rose above the trees.

Ayden had heard this conversation before.

Behind him, the cicadas' monotonous call fell silent. Curious, he twisted to look over his shoulder, across the rutted road, and into the darkness beneath the foliage.

Both sides of the road were heavily wooded, and he had noticed plenty of deer and smaller animals as they traveled between the towns today.

Somehow, he sensed this was different.

This was hunger on four legs, moving in a pack.

From the shadows, golden eyes reflected firelight. At first, there were two, then four, then eight.

His parents murmured about their uncertain future beside the fire, unaware of the threat.

The magical skills practiced by his parents and the adults in their old coven were confusing and varied. Different from ordinary people, witches, like his family, developed their skills near puberty. These skills allowed them to manipulate elemental forces—*Water, Earth, Fire,* and *Air.* Two centuries ago, innocent people were burned at the stake, charged with being a witch. Ayden found that fact both sad and amusing. Normal humans could never burn a witch who controlled the *elements*. Those witch hunters could have only murdered their own kind.

The visions in the fire were new to him, as was the touch of feral minds—wolves that lurked in the trees across the road. Pack desire fed their urgency, and Ayden sensed their resolve to strike.

There's nothing for you here.

His palm held out to the wolves, Ayden gave his thought a form, not unlike the images he watched within the fire, then opened himself to the canine minds across the road.

No food for the pack here, only fire and pain.

He thought of the deer he'd seen jump between trees a few hours ago and projected that memory across the road to the pack leader.

Take your family to this place. Hunt there.

One by one, the shining eyes blinked shut until only silence stalked the other side of the road. In moments, the cicadas resumed their shrill song.

Ayden turned his back on the darkness. The sleepiness from moments before had burned away in the excitement over his evolving *elemental-skills*.

I have the same type of earth-magic Father has!

His father's way with animals made him one of the best farriers in New Haven, but cheaper labor had won over his employer.

Ayden pulled on his britches, and crawled from beneath the wagon, anxious to share his new skill with his parents.

His mother and father turned at the sound of his steps.

"Did we wake you?" his father asked.

"No." Ayden moved to sit beside his mother, but movement in the fire caught and held his attention.

"Then what is it, Ayden?" His mother took his hand and urged him to take a seat. "Are you hungry?"

Ayden shook his head, mesmerized by the events transpiring in the flame. "I'm going to have a baby brother," he whispered, eyes wide, transfixed by the scene before him.

"What gave you that idea, son?" His father tossed a stick into the fire.

"I can see him." Ayden looked to his father. "You're holding him in your arms, and there's snow falling outside the window."

His parents exchanged guarded glances.

"What makes you say this, sweetheart?" His mother touched his shoulder. "Did you have a dream?"

Ayden's gaze remained fixed on the small blaze. "No. It's in the fire. I can see it now." He pointed at the dancing flames, low and flickering along the top of the evening's last log. "I've seen people in the fire before, but no one I know, and never this clear." He looked at his mother. "Can you do this?"

"No, darling. Divination, if that is what this truly is—is an uncommon ability—a type of *spirit-magic,* unrelated to our *elemental-skills.*"

"Is your—" His father hesitated and swallowed. "Do you see your mother? Is she with us? Try to remember even the smallest of details."

Ayden's eyes darted to the vision in the flame. The center, where his father held the now swaddled baby, was clear, but the edges faded into the fire. "I don't see you, mama." He tried harder, but the vision became shadows and then empty flames. He shook his head. "It's just a fire now."

"It's all right, Ayden." His mother gathered him into a hug.

Ayden would have pushed away from hugs and affection, but right this minute, he wanted the comfort of his mother's arms. "I can try again." He stretched to see the campfire clearly, but his father snuffed the flames with a small gesture.

"You can try tomorrow night. Now, back to bed with you. We want an early start."

"Yes, sir." Ayden gave his father a quick hug then hurried to his blankets.

His father steadied his mother as she rose and crossed the dark campground. At the other wagon, he gave her a foot up.

Ayden had just closed his eyes when he remembered the wolves and the other skill he had discovered. He rose onto his elbow, squinting in the dark at the wagon where his parents slept.

I'll tell them tomorrow.

He thought he would dream of wolves, but instead, his dreams were of the images he'd seen that night in the fire.

By sunrise, the wagons were hitched with one horse each and rolled toward Boston. Ayden held the reins of the second wagon, seated beside his mother, while his father took the lead with the wagon hauling their furniture.

"How long have you had visions in the fire?" His mother rocked with the dips in the rutted road beside him.

"A few weeks, I think. I thought they were dreams." Ayden glanced at his mother, and she smiled.

"The ability to see visions in fire is called pyromancy. It's quite rare. I've known a few witches who use water to scry for omens, and I've heard of others whose visions come to them in dreams, but I've never known one who could read portends in fire." She patted his leg. "Knowledge of the future is not always a blessing. You must always consider how much you wish to share about what you see."

They stopped for lunch beside a stream, then following the directions provided by their former coven leader, continued to the Brown farm.

A small yellow dog announced their arrival from the wooden porch, and a half-dozen chickens scattered across the yard as the lead wagon pulled to a stop.

Ayden drew the second buckboard close beside it. "Whoa."

The curtains at the front window moved, then the door opened. A man, his father's age, stepped onto the porch. "Can I help you?" The glass of his wire-rimmed spectacles sparkled in the afternoon light. The tanned skin on his face and forehead stopped at a line marking the edge of where his hat had protected his white-skinned receding hairline.

"I hope so," his father replied from his seat on the wagon. "We are looking for a Mr. Garrett Brown."

"You found him. I'm Garrett Brown. And you are?"

"My name is Lyam MacKenna." He indicated the second wagon. "My wife, Rachael, and my son, Ayden." Lyam did not step down from the wagon but remained seated. "We've recently departed from New Haven. Before we left, a close friend of ours, Louis Franklin, suggested we might stop at your farm on our way into Boston. He asked that we give you his regards."

Farmer Brown's eyebrows rose. "Cousin Lou? How's he getting on? It's been a good five years since I've seen him."

His father chuckled. "Mr. Franklin remembers your custard pudding from last Christmas fondly."

"So, he does." The farmer grinned. "If Lou sent you to me, then I have a good idea why you've come. Please, tie off your reins and come inside. I have cider cooling in the icebox."

"Thank you, but we can't stay long." Lyam tied the reins to the tall hand brake and climbed down from the wagon. He nodded for Ayden to do the same. "We'll need to find temporary lodging in town. I doubt they'll allow us to camp on the side of the street."

Ayden jumped to the ground and helped his mother down from the buckboard seat.

"No," the farmer chuckled. "That won't do." He held his arm wide, welcoming Ayden and his mother. "I think we can do better than sleeping rough by the road." He quickly scanned the yard then called out in a loud voice, "Boys! Come take care of these horses."

"You have children?" Rachael asked.

"Oh, no. They're not mine. I never married." Garrett smiled as identical twin boys raced around the side of the house. "These two belong to one of my—families. They turned fourteen at the end of June, and their mother thought it a good idea to give her city boys a taste of country living." He nodded with pride as the twins hurried up to the geldings. "They've been with me almost a month, helping with farm chores and learning to make simple furniture items in my barn woodshop."

"How kind of you to take them in." Rachael stepped onto the porch as Mr. Brown opened the door.

"Not at all. It's good to have the boys here."

Ayden's parents preceded the farmer into his home.

Brown paused in the doorway and looked back at Ayden. "You're welcome to join your parents inside, young man. If you like."

Ayden nodded climbed the wooden step to the porch.

The farmer glanced over at the twins and then followed Ayden's parents into the house.

Ayden hesitated at the door as he watched the youngsters hurry to their task.

Except for the color of their shirts, the boys attending to the horses were identical. Barefoot, their khaki-colored trousers rolled up to below their knees, and their dark brown hair hanging in their eyes.

The boy beside the first wagon climbed onto the seat, took the reins, released the brake, then addressed Ayden. "If the horses are to stay hitched, they'll be easier to water in the back."

"—at the long troughs," the brother finished and climbed onto Ayden's wagon.

"All right," Ayden replied. "I'll let my folks know."

The older boys paused for a split second, and then they nodded in unison.

Ayden watched until the second wagon disappeared around the side of the farmhouse.

Identical twins!

He'd never imagined such a thing. And they were close to his age. If his parents were to join Farmer Brown's coven, then they might become his friends.

I wonder what magic they already know.

Inside the farmhouse, Ayden followed the voices down a short hallway and paused at the kitchen door.

"It would be no imposition for me, I assure you." He poured an extra glass of chilled water, nodded to Ayden, and put the glass before the chair closest to the door, then returned the pitcher to the icebox. "We have a *gathering* set for the twentieth. That's just a few days away. The twins will return to Boston with their parents the day after." He took a seat at the table across from Lyam. "I would be honored to have you stay with me until then. Goddess knows I've got the room." He sipped from his glass and raised a brow at Ayden, who stood in the doorway and nodded toward an empty chair. "Many who'll attend live in Boston. They may know of an opening for a farrier at an inn, or livery, or even with a blacksmith."

Ayden took his seat at the table and sipped the cool water. "Will there be more children?"

"Your age, you mean?" Brown nodded. "The twins have a younger sister, and there are probably four or five others close to your age which will come with their parents." He spoke across the table to Lyam and Rachael. "I've two barns in back. The largest I keep empty for *gatherings*. The meetings are for coven members and special guests only." He smiled at Ayden. "But you'll have plenty of new friends to keep you entertained while the adults meet."

Chapter 2

Chantal James

—

August 2, 1841 - Beacon Hill

Chantal awoke from the dream with a gasp.

Beside her, the familiar soft snore of her husband, Sully, continued undisturbed.

Outside the window, the full August moon sailed peacefully through a cloudless early morning sky.

Tonight, they would gather beneath the coven moon.

Perspiration dotted her forehead, and she turned her damp pillow over before she sank back down and stared sightlessly at the moonlight cast upon the wall. Afraid to close her eyes and slip back into the familiar nightmare. More of a memory of a night much like this.

It would have been a full moon then too.

Chantal's eyes fluttered closed, and as she feared, she reentered her dream.

***

Young and naïve, she stood in her dark hooded robe, hands raised in supplication. The coven chanted their response to the request spoken by their High Priest for the four sacred corners and the Lord and Lady to hear their prayers.

Married for a month, since the last coven gathering, she imagined she could feel the touch of Sully's hand as the coarse cotton robe brushed her nipple and along her thigh, and she grinned.

The girl beside her would be inducted into the coven tonight. Her skills blended with those of her brother and sister witches. She would be one with them.

But the girl stumbled.

What was her name?

The fallen girl didn't right herself to continue in the circle. Instead, she collapses to the ground, her back arched and her limbs shaking.

A seizure!

Chantal fell to her knees beside the girl as she half-rose, then crumpled. Her eyes roll back in her head while her heels beat a tattoo on the floor. Her lips moved, and foam from her throat dripped from the side of her mouth.

What is she trying to say?

Chantal looked to the faces around her for help, but the shadow of their hoods concealed their identities.

No! That's not how it happened.

—

Six coven members had volunteered to visit the family after the monthly gathering. Their wagon arrived near dawn and entered the young woman's bedchamber.

The sickroom smelled of stale urine and vomit.

The girl lay quiet as they shuffled in, filing into the small room along the wall by the bedside. First in line, Chantal stood next to the nightstand at the head of the bed.

As they chanted a healing prayer, the trembling began in the young woman's arms and legs and increased until she thrashed beneath the covers.

High Priest Garrett Brown stepped up, called the corner elements in a clear voice, and cast a *Circle of Protection*.

Garrett wasn't the High Priest. He wasn't even there.

I must be dreaming.

"Ya Yar. Yoouu," the girl in the bed uttered from deep in her throat, back arched, her hands stiffened into claws.

"Can someone help me?" Chantal glanced over her shoulder at the hooded group as she held the girl's shoulders to the bed. When she looked back down, the girl's green eyes stared into hers.

The youngster's voice garbled and stuttering before now rang soft but clear. Froth ran from the side of her mouth into her hair. "You will know them by their birth—crowned beneath a full moon on the witches' High Sabbat."

"Sully?" Panic fired in the pit of Chantal's stomach.

Why won't anyone help me? Where's Sully?

"Their *twyne* shall wake the Demon," the girl smiled.

"No, no, no, no...." Chantal released the girl and held her hands over her ears.

Not again.

"By Fire and Earth, he shall be felled—lest the *twyne* fail—then death shall reign."

—

A scream tore from Chantal's throat as remembered pain ripped her asunder.

"You're almost there, Mrs. James. One more good effort." The midwife touched her thigh with warm hands. "Take a deep breath, and now push."

She bore down and forced the first baby from her womb.

"You are truly blessed. There is another child, bear down one more time, and you're done."

Twins.

Born under the waning crescent moon with the deep January snow outside, her twins were spared the horror of the prophecy.

But the dying witch spoke directly to me.

A scream tore from Chantal's throat as the agony of childbirth tore through her a second time.

***

"Chantal!" Sully pressed her shoulders into the bed and shook her. "Wake up. You're dreaming again."

Chilled and drenched in sweat, Chantal heard Sully's beloved voice and struggled from her slumber. Early morning light filled the room, and her husband's searching eyes stared down into hers. "I'm sorry, Sully. I'm so sorry."

"Are you better now? Was it the same dream?" Sully ran his hands down her nightgown-covered arms and lifted her hands to his lips to kiss her knuckles. "I thought the nightmares were getting better."

"They are—were." She sat up in bed. "It's the full moon." She pushed her nails across her scalp and gave what she hoped was an encouraging smile to Sully.

"And the gathering is tonight. I do understand." He tugged the pull for the maid. "Have the girl bring you some tea. Today will linger far into tomorrow for us both." Sully put a robe on and winked as he left their room.

Chantal lay back and played with the ends of her hair, still dark brown except for the white lock that fell from her forehead.

From the shock of that girl dying in my arms and then my giving birth to twins.

"You rang, ma'am?" A young dark-haired servant looked around the partially open door. Her blue mop cap hid the remainder of her tresses.

"Yes. Tea and a biscuit, please, then I need to dress." Chantal stretched and slid her legs from beneath the covers and touched the floor with her toes.

With a bob of the mop cap, the youthful face disappeared.

The ache in her back, a remnant of the back labor of her dream, twinged. She pressed the heel of her palm against her side and leaned into the pain. Sully had been correct. Today would be an exceptionally long day.

By late morning, their travel trunks were packed for the trip to the Brown farm. She'd had new robes made for her and Sully and another set for her twins, Bernard and Bayard, who would join the coven in a formal ritual tonight.

Ready to depart, Chantal hesitated at the window and watched her young daughter play in the garden below.

Margaret occupied herself, without enthusiasm, with her new doll in the afternoon sunlight as the neighbor lad looked on.

The neighbor boy, Robert Prescott, was the same age as Margaret, only eleven years old. The two had been fast friends for most of their young lives. His dark head bent toward Margaret's auburn curls in whispered conversations. One was never far from the other.

Chantal should have expected as much from her daughter.

Margaret, a tomboy through and through, with dusty skirts and tangled hair as evidence, would naturally befriend one of the neighborhood lads rather than a girl. Margaret's older brothers had no time for children their own age, much less a nuisance of a younger sister.

Still, this childhood friendship between her daughter and Robert would never be allowed to blossom into more than playmates. Margaret would be an adult witch soon. A young woman imbued with powerful magic, like the rest of her family. As a coven member, she would never be allowed to wed an unskilled human.

Still—the Prescott family is a member of the Boston Brahmins as we are.

Chantal had time to decide on her daughter's future and guide Margaret's choices in all things—to be sure her match would be with one of their kind, either witch or social equal. If a proper suitor materialized, he would be scrutinized.

There is always The Prophecy to consider, after all.

"Are you ready?" Sully asked from the doorway.

Chantal turned to her husband with a thoughtful smile. "I am."

Sully held out his arms to either side. "How do I look? Dapper enough to be seen with such a beautiful woman?"

Chantal chuckled as she rolled her eyes.

Sullivan James would be considered elegant enough for any woman. His fine brown hair glinted with silver, and laughing dark eyes crinkled at the corners in a loveable familiar way. Sully had been her rock, her husband, and the father of her four children for twenty-five years if you count the child they lost. Sully could still make her laugh and lighten the dark and protective side of her nature.

He'd heard *The Prophecy of the Twins* spoken of on the same night she had, but those words didn't writhe inside him as they did her. The only thing that saved her sanity was that her twins' birth took place beneath a crescent moon and not on a solstice, as foretold in the dreadful prophecy.

She would never forget the young woman's dying words. They shocked the entire coven. And although the ominous prediction haunted her then, it became an absolute obsession after the birth of her sons.

As twin witches, they could merge their consciousness by *twyning*—one of the first skills her boys displayed at far too young an age.

Sully shrugged off the birth of his children with any connection to the prophecy, especially since they failed to meet the prophecy's requirements.

But Chantal knew prophecies were tricky things to interpret at best.

And Sully never gave birth to a child.

She put the thought away and smiled at her husband. "You're dashing, as always, Mr. James." She let the curtain fall shut and held out her hand. "A coven moon is on the rise, and we bring our boys home tomorrow."

Sully kissed the back of her gloved hand. "Speaking of the coven, we should be on our way. It's a four-hour ride to Brown's barn at least." He looked around the room in mock confusion. "Where is our little one? Won't she accompany us?"

"You know she will." Chantal grinned despite her dark thoughts. "Margaret's dressed and ready, playing with Robert in the garden, as usual. Bern and Bay can keep an eye on her before their induction ceremony if need be."

"They'll be pleased with that." A sarcastic half-grin flashed across Sully's face as he wrapped her hand around the inside of his arm.

"They're good boys. They'll do as they're told."

Sully held her arm as they descended the stairs.

The housemaid stood waiting with her mistress's sunbonnet beside the door.

"Our bags are in the wagon?" Chantal took the bonnet and arranged it over her hair, tying the gauze ribbons beneath her chin, and looked over the selections of parasols in the stand.

"Yes, ma'am." The maid bobbed her head, eyes steady on the floor.

"Please fetch Miss Margaret." Sully directed the maid. He opened the door and followed Chantal onto the stoop of their Beacon Hill home, then paused, turning back to the servant. "She's in the garden. Tell her to come along. It's time to go."

"Yes, Mr. James." The maid hurried through the long narrow house toward the back garden.

The groom held the reins to the single horse-drawn buckboard that waited on the cobblestone street at the end of the walk.

Chantal swished her skirt in irritation. "Next month, the boys can follow in the wagon, and we will ride in the covered trap."

"Yes, dear," Sully quipped as he helped her climb to the high seat.

Chantal glanced into the back of the wagon and nodded with satisfaction that their overnight luggage and hooded robes were loaded. Blankets stacked along the side would cushion the ride for the children.

Sully took the reins from the groom and climbed onto the seat beside Chantal.

Moments later, Margaret burst out the door and ran down the walk. The bows in her dark auburn hair had come undone and flapped down her back.

The groom helped her into the back of the wagon. She stepped around the trunks and settled on a double stack of blankets near her parents.

"Did you forget your doll?" Sully asked.

"No, Papa. I left her with Robbie." She shrugged and looked between her parents to the street ahead. "I don't play with dolls as much as I used to, and I know he'll take good care of her."

Chantal exchanged a significant glance with Sully. "They grow up too fast," she spoke under her breath.

"They certainly do."

An hour from the Brown farm, the cart horse began to favor his left front leg.

"Damn," Sully muttered and pulled back on the reins, guiding the animal to a halt in the road.

"What happened?" Rubbing her eyes, Margaret sat up from her nest of blankets.

"Jack may have picked up a rock." Sully handed his wife the reins and jumped to the ground.

"Does he have a stone?" Chantal leaned to the side to get a better view.

Sully patted Jack's neck and ran a hand down the horse's left front leg, then lifted the foot. "No. Not at all. The farrier did a poor job of trimming his hooves. The shoe couldn't have sat flat. It's a wonder he isn't lame." He circled the horse and checked each hoof. "They all need to be trimmed and reshod." He paced several yards down the road and stood staring back the way they had come, hands on his hips, inhaling deeply.

The warm late afternoon was heavy with humidity since they'd turned inland. Sully had abandoned his jacket an hour ago, and his white cotton shirt clung to the sweat on his back.

"Do we turn back then?" Chantal asked with dismay. She didn't relish a three-hour return trip in this heat. She rested the parasol on her shoulder, her back to the west.

Sully shook his head as he turned and pushed damp hair from his brow. "We're closer to Garrett's than home."

"He doesn't have a blacksmith at the farm, does he?"

"No, but I wager he'll have a hoof nipper and rasp. I can take the remaining shoes off and trim Jack's hooves." He climbed onto the seat and took the reins. "I'd take them off now if I had the right tools, but we're almost to the farm." He shook the reins, and the gelding stepped forward, still favoring his leg. "Jack can take us home barefoot tomorrow. It will be fine."

***

A coven gathering always brought bedlam to Garrett's farm. Today was no different.

Sully guided Jack between two carriages halted on either side of the drive, their horses already unhitched and led to Garrett's big corral in back. Caring for the coven's animals fell to the older children.

An almost carnival atmosphere prevailed, with the younger children squealing with excitement near the front porch and the slightly older boys and girls playing hide and seek in the tall cornrows.

"This is always fun." Chantal smiled at the friendly chaos.

Sully reined Jack off the road as Bernard hurried up to his father's side of the wagon.

"Hello, son." Sully mussed Bernard's hair and chuckled at his son's indignant look. "Poor Jack threw a shoe." He handed Bernard the reins as the two exchanged places. "The other shoes need to be removed and his hooves trimmed before we head back to Boston."

"Is he injured?" Bern settled into the buckboard seat, holding Jack steady.

Sully shook his head. "No. He's fine. Where's Garrett?

"In back, getting people settled."

Sully exchanged a glance with Chantal before he paced away.

Bayard helped his mother down from the wagon. "Hello, mum."

"Bay." Chantal embraced him lightly then pulled back. "Did you enjoy your stay at the farm?"

"I did." The grin stayed on his face as he hurried to the back of the wagon and held out his arms to Margaret. "But we had to go to bed far too early."

"Thank you, Bay," Margaret held his shoulders as he helped her from the wagon.

"What did you think, Bernard?" Chantal's motherly gaze settled on her oldest twin.

Bernard gazed back for a moment. "I missed our pies."

Chantal laughed despite Bernard's serious demeanor. "There is an apple turnover with your name on it as soon as we get home."

Sully and Garrett rounded the main house, and Sully pointed to their rig. "...and all four hooves need reshoeing."

Garrett nodded a greeting to Chantal as he continued to the James' horse. He ran a hand down the left front leg and examined the hoof. "You know I don't believe in luck or coincidence, but I have a farrier and his family staying at the farm."

"You have house guests?" Chantal rounded the horse. Her parasol gripped tightly in her gloved hand. Her voice dropped to a low hiss, "With the gathering tonight, have you taken leave of your senses?"

"Actually—" Garrett straightened from his inspection of the horse and stepped forward. His gaze met the tall woman's accusation directly. "They're

newcomers from New Haven." He chuckled and winked at Bayard. "The father is looking for work in Boston. I invited them to stay—" he held his finger
up as Chantal began to speak, "—and *participate* in our gathering ceremonies
if they so choose. It is a chance for them to meet our coven members, many of
whom live in Boston and may know of an opening for a farrier in town."

"Your guests are *skilled* then." Chantal shook the dust from the edge of her
skirt. "You could have mentioned that first thing."

"I could have, but your need is for a farrier. Of witches, we have more than
enough." Garrett stared a moment longer at Chantal, then turned to Sully.
"Have your boys unhitch your animal and bring him to the corral in back. I'm
sure Mr. MacKenna would be happy to look at your beast and take care of the
issue. Did you find the shoe...?" The two men walked as they spoke, and their
voices faded as they rounded the farmhouse.

Bayard had already released two straps holding the wagon forks to either
side of the gelding.

Bernard held Jack still while the two boys communicated silently. When
the last buckle came free, Bernard tossed his brother the reins then dropped
from the wagon. "I'm taking Jack to the corral," the boys intoned in unison.

A tug on Chantal's dress drew her attention. "I'm sorry, did you need something, Margaret?"

"Yes, Mama. I asked if I could go play in the field with the others."

Several children scampered and called to one another at the edge of the
cornfield. Garrett's corn rose above most adult's heads. To the youngsters, the
aisles of corn became a vast game of hide-and-seek.

"Stay near the edge and come when your brothers call you for supper."
Chantal reached to straighten Margaret's ribbons, but her daughter had already dashed away across the wide oval drive.

***

Margaret James

—

A dark-haired boy she didn't recognize caught Margaret's attention as their wagon emerged from the wooded road and into the open drive at the front of Mr. Brown's farmhouse.

Along the far side of the clearing, rows of corn, over six-foot-high, stretched into the distance. Familiar faces Margaret saw once a month, twice if there was a High Sabbat or a blue moon, called to each other as they ran down the rows of corn just beginning to silk.

The strange boy stood alone near the field's edge and appeared unsure if he should include himself in the hiding game. His gaze circled the wide clearing as he shifted from foot to foot, and he glanced over his shoulder toward the big corral in back.

Margaret knew where the corral stood.

She knew this farm.

She did not know the boy but understood his dilemma.

Too old for a child's game but not old enough to be comfortable with the teenagers who helped with the coven gathering.

Older like my brothers. Or Gordon and Milton, Ugh!

As though her thought had conjured them, the twins rounded the farmhouse and ran toward their wagon.

Her gaze returned to the new boy.

Hands shoved deep in his trouser pockets, he turned his attention from the back of the farmhouse and looked across the numerous wagons left haphazardly along the long farm drive.

He saw her watching him, and the sweep of his observation stopped as they stared at one another.

Bay leaned into her field of vision and held out his arms while replying to their mother. "But we had to go to bed far too early."

"Thank you, Bay," Margaret put her hands on her brother's shoulders and hopped to the ground.

Bay steadied her landing then hurried to the wagon's front with Bernard and their father.

Half listening to her elder's conversation, she watched the children play beside the corn. Her regular *moon-friends* were seated in a circle near the front porch, holding their baby dolls and pretending to drink tea. For a moment, a pang of loss tightened her throat, and she wished for the dolly she'd left with Robert.

Her attention wandered back to the game of tag near the cornfield. The dark-haired boy's regard waited, and a small knowing smile lifted his lips. "Can I go play, Mama?" She tore her gaze from the boy and looked up.

Her mother stared with narrowed eyes at Mr. Brown and Papa as the two men hurried around the farmhouse, heads close in a discussion.

Margaret tugged on her mother's dress.

"I'm sorry, did you need something, Margaret?"

"Yes, Mama. I asked if I could play in the cornfield with the others."

Her mother's eyes raked the field, and her head dipped in approval.

Margaret sped away at a run.

"Stay near the edge..." her mother's voice faded as she raced toward the boy she found so compelling. Shyness slowed her pace as she approached, but at that instant, he grinned again.

She beamed back and halted before him. "Hi." Nervousness struggled against something strange and unnamed.

A dark lock of hair hung across his brow, and his eyes sparkled with delight as he stared into hers. He shook his head slowly from side to side. "I've seen this before, you know." His tanned hand pushed the hair back from his face. "It was you. I'm sure of it."

"That's impossible," Margaret challenged. "When did you see me?"

"A week ago, maybe." He scrubbed at his face and spun around on his heel, arms thrown as wide as his grin. His attention whirled away from her. "This proves it's true."

"What's true?" She yanked on his shirt sleeve. "You should try to make sense when you meet someone new." She waited until he looked back at her. "How do you do? I'm Margaret James."

"Pleased to meet you, Margaret James. Now I have a name to put to the face." Still grinning, he tipped his head in a slight bow. "I'm Ayden MacKenna."

"What do you mean? Explain yourself. Where did you see me before?"

He looked over his shoulder then leaned forward as though to impart a secret. "I see things—things that are going to happen. The first thing I ever saw was you, running toward me across the way there." He swung his arm, pointing toward her family wagon. "It was your face I saw in the fire."

Chapter 3

Chantal James

—

Chantal sighed with aggravation and brushed at the wrinkles on her skirt. She raised her chin to catch the delicate hint of a cool breeze. Her gaze followed Margaret as she skipped to a halt in front of a young man Chantal didn't recognize. The youngster appeared to be roughly the same age as her twins.

On the far side of the farmhouse, three boys she did recognize, children of other coven members, strode purposefully toward the stranger and her daughter.

Along the corn row's edge, a half-dozen children shrieked and called out to one another.

A typical gathering. Nothing of concern.

She hurried after the twins. As soon as they finished with Jack, she'd have them set up their family tent in the fallow field behind the barns. Most of the best locations were probably already taken.

Near the large cook pit in the center of the massive backyard, Sully and the newcomer spoke from either side of Garrett Brown. The farrier stood as tall as her husband, who she knew to be just over six foot. With dark hair and eyes, Garrett's guest appeared as a larger version of the boy she'd seen with her daughter.

As Chantal approached the men, Sully shook the stranger's hand, and they both tipped their heads in agreement.

The farrier spoke briefly to Garrett, and then he followed the twins and Jack into the shadow of the closest building.

"I take it that's your New Haven farrier and that he can see to Jack." Chantal came to a stop beside her husband and surveyed the roasting pit. "Will he have time to correct the hooves before dinner?"

"I think so," Sully replied. "Lyam understands what's needed and has his own tools."

"Marvelous. Can I have the boys set up our tent before we eat?" The large canvas tent would act as a dressing area where she and Sully could don their robes before midnight. After the ceremony, the family would use the shelter to rest for several hours before returning to Boston the next day.

"I don't see why not." Sully turned his smiling demeanor to Garrett. "Unless you require them?"

"No. Your boys should help you get settled." Garrett indicated three young men leading more horses to the corral. "I've plenty of help for the time being, but I'll be sorry to see your young men go home."

"I hope they haven't caused you too much trouble," Chantal took Sully's arm as they walked with Garrett to the house.

"No trouble at all. Your children are marvelous youngsters. You should be very proud." Garrett led them onto the wide wrap-around veranda and indicated several empty chairs. "Please, have a seat. There are cool drinks in the kitchen, sweet lemonade and apple cider, a variety of whiskey and rum drinks, and wine. Dinner should be ready shortly after sundown. Now, if you'll excuse me, I must see to the other guests who have arrived."

"Thank you, Garrett." Chantal nodded to their host and pointed at a small table with two chairs near the porch rail. "Let's sit there."

"Would you like lemonade?" Sully asked.

"Yes. Thank you."

"I'll be right back."

Chantal smiled at her husband, gathered her skirts, and settled into a simple wooden chair. She waved her gloved fingers at two women at the table across from her. "Lovely to see you again."

The women responded in kind then went back to their conversation.

Chantal looked across the chaos that had descended on Garrett's normally quiet farm. His mid-sized coven included fifteen or so active members, many of whom regularly brought their children to the gatherings. Older children would watch the younger ones while the adults attended the monthly rituals.

Pleasantries with the women attended to, Chantal gazed at the slant of the late afternoon sunshine between Garrett's two large barns. A long golden beam fell between the buildings and bathed the roasting pit in light.

Several people stood in the sunshine beside the firepit while two men tested the doneness of the roasted pig on the spit. Nods and a few cheers told her the pork was ready.

Without setting a foot inside, Chantal knew a long table with offerings from each family would fill the dinner plates of the gathering. Her family never brought a dish. Instead, she and Sully's contribution to the coven included the farm itself, along with everything else Garrett required to see him through to the next full moon.

Sully set a glass of lemonade on the table before her and sipped his whiskey. "Lyam MacKenna, the new farrier, will be done with Jack before midnight." He took another sip then placed his drink on the table. He slipped out of his jacket, hanging the garment over the back of his chair, then unhooked his cufflinks from their kissing cuffs and slid the jewelry into his pocket before he rolled up the sleeve. "It's warm."

The tart drink left a tingle on her lips. "I wonder who made the lemonade?" She glanced at the table across from her, but the ladies had vacated their seats.

In the yard, several guests shook out large blankets for a family picnic.

"I want the tent set up before the boys' sup," Chantal instructed, shaking a finger toward the barn.

The twins emerged from the shadowed interior. Their noses pointed directly toward the cooked pork, being carved or shredded into large bowls.

"I'll help them." Spotting his sons, Sully hopped over the three steps to the veranda and jogged toward the boys. Gathering their attention, Sully gave brief instructions, then Bern and Bay ran toward the front of the house, and Sully headed toward the field.

The twins waved to Chantal as they ran past the veranda and headed to the wagon to retrieve the tent and bedding.

Half a glass of lemonade later, they reappeared, the heavy canvas tent slung between them. Margaret and the new boy—something MacKenna—followed behind. Her daughter carried their canvas bags and several blankets, and her new friend lugged Sully's old trunk, where the cloaks and ritual items were packed.

Coven members and their families migrated from around the farm to the hard-packed dirt yard. Two women hurried from the house with a stack of metal plates, and the loud clang-clang-clang of the dinner bell rang at the front of the house.

***

Margaret James

—

Margaret narrowed her eyes as she and the new boy stood nose to nose, him grinning like a fool. "Do you think I'm stupid?"

"No." He stepped back, and his smile faded. "Do you think I'm lying?"

Margaret shrugged. "I've never heard of anything like that before, is all. Is your element fire?"

Ayden shook his head. "No. Well, I don't know, but I don't think so. I haven't tried to use fire."

"You should." Margaret lowered her voice, "You might be a mighty *fire-mage*. Have you manifested anything at all?"

"I, uh—*Earth*, like my father. An affinity for animals."

"*Fire* and *Earth*? You might be a healer." Margaret nodded.

"My mother can heal small wounds."

"You might take after her."

"Have you manifested?" Ayden asked.

"Well, I—oof!"

Eyes wide with surprise, Ayden stumbled forward and bumped her nose hard with his chest. He knocked her to the ground then landed almost on top of her.

"Oh look, Little Miss James has a boyfriend," Gordy Carmichael snickered.

"Better not get caught with her, or the twins will make sure you disappear for good," Gordon's sidekick Milty Kohler chimed in.

Ayden rolled to the side and sat up. "Why would you push me?" he demanded.

"The new boy likes Maggie," Gordy taunted her, then sneered at Ayden, "What're you going to do about it?" Closer in age to Margaret's brothers, Gordon cupped his hand, and a flicker of fire appeared above his fingers. "I'm not afraid of the sideshow twins." He smirked while he admired the fire in his hand.

"You should be." Margaret scrambled to her feet and brushed at the dust on her skirt. "They'll fry your guts, Gordon Carmichael."

"No, they won't—Ow!" A stone ricocheted off the back of his hand, knocking the flame from his palm. Gordon clutched the injury and spun on his heel to look for the attacker.

Milty took a step back, his eyes darting around the clearing.

Margaret glanced down at Ayden, still on the ground.

His eyes remained sharp on the bullies while his fingers caressed an egg-size stone.

Margaret took a step forward, placing herself between Ayden and the older boys, hands on her hips.

Gordon won't harm me because of my brothers, but they'd hurt the new boy.

"You better run," she taunted. "Bern and Bay will be here any minute, I'll tell them what you did, and you'll be dead."

"Oh yeah?" The older boy's head swung back to Margaret and narrowed his eyes.

The sudden sharp clang of the dinner bell startled Margaret, but she kept her gaze firmly on her adversary.

"We'll see you lovebirds later." Gordon slapped Milty on the back, and they strode toward the back of the farmhouse and dinner.

"I know I'm not supposed to hate, but those two—" Margaret watched just in case they turned back.

"You won't get an argument from me." Ayden stood beside her. "My mom says people who are cruel learned to be that way by being hurt by someone else."

"He would have hurt you if he knew you threw the rock." She walked beside him toward the farmhouse.

"I didn't *throw* it," Ayden declared proudly.

"No?"

"The one in my hand was just in case I needed to."

Chapter 4

Ayden MacKenna

—

Ayden claimed one of the haybales arranged between the cooking pit and the tables, far enough to be away from the heat but with a clear view of the flame. He'd filled his tin plate with a roasted chicken leg and thigh, baked beans, and cooked carrots and potatoes.

Most folks ate at tables on the wide veranda. However, Ayden's mother and father ate on a shared haybale across the firepit from him.

"Can I sit with you?" Margaret waited, plate in hand, for him to respond.

"Sure." Ayden gestured to a bale angled close to his. "So, what happens tonight?"

"Ah," Margaret took a bite of her chicken leg, chewed, and swallowed before answering. "After we eat and the latecomers finish setting up their tents, the coven members change into their ceremonial robes. Near midnight, they will enter the big barn over there and close the doors." She stirred her beans with a tin fork. "My brothers are joining the coven tonight."

"They weren't members before?"

"No. You have to be an adult or manifest well enough to be tested by the leader to name your skill discipline."

"Oh." He sucked on the end of the chicken bone and scanned the gathering. The bullies, and several other young people, ate on the far side of the yard, close to the big barn.

Garrett Brown rose from a blanket and strolled to the fire. He tossed his chicken bones into the blaze then set his dinner-tin on the stones that encircled the pit. Hands in his back pockets, the coven leader surveyed the people gathered between his house and the barns. "What is tonight?" he asked. His gaze touched several children with their parents as he turned to address the gathering.

"The full moon," a boy called back.

"Well, that's true. But it was full last night as well and will be full again tomorrow night. Why is tonight different?"

"Because the moon is full all day too, even if we can't see it." A young girl sank to her knees on a blanket near where Mr. Brown spoke.

"That's right. Does anyone know what we call this full moon, this special day in the full moon cycle?"

"The Coven Moon," several children called back.

Laughter erupted around the gathering. Conversations dwindled as even the adults quieted to listen to the leader speak.

"The Coven Moon is a special night for us. We gather as a family, like-minded individuals with similar skills, to give thanks to the Lord and Lady for the gifts within us—and around us." He ruffled a lad's hair as he walked among his guests, then worked his way back to the firepit while he spoke. "Tonight will be even more special as we welcome new members to our coven. Bernard and Bayard James. These young men, who have matured enough to manifest their *elemental-skills*, will be tested tonight to determine their major and minor disciplines."

The children of the coven had inched their way forward and sat wide-eyed around Leader Brown.

"Who knows how many elements a witch can manipulate?"

Several hands rose while several more voices chimed, "Four."

"Correct. The spirits we call to guard our circle—*Fire, Earth, Air,* and *Water*—gift us with the ability to manipulate their elements." A dynamic speaker, Garrett Brown, held the attention of the children as well as their elders.

The sun slipped below the horizon while the leader spoke to the children.

The full moon rose big and bold in the eastern sky and cast a milky light across the diners.

In the deep shadow below the veranda, Margaret's brothers ate on the ground near where their parents were seated.

Margaret's father rose, stepped down into the yard, and wove his way through the blankets and haybales toward Ayden's father.

"What happens after the barn doors close? Do you know?" Ayden whispered to Margaret.

She shrugged and leaned close to whisper back, "Mama said they pray to the Goddess and give thanks and stuff."

Sully James spoke to Ayden's father, and then they both chuckled and spoke briefly with his mother. In the end, the men left their empty plates on the stones around the pit with Leader Brown's and headed to the working barn.

As they walked past Ayden and Margaret, neither man acknowledged the children before disappearing into the outbuilding.

"Your father is going to fix the shoes on our horse."

Ayden gazed for a moment at Margaret before he spoke. "What's wrong with them?"

Margaret licked the grease from the chicken off her fingers and shrugged. "He lost a shoe, and the rest are bad."

"My dad is good with horses and owns his tools." Ayden nodded. "He'll fix the problem." When he turned back to the gathering, his attention caught on the fire burning low in the pit. White-hot embers glowed orange as blue-tipped flames rose and fell.

Shadows spun and narrowed, becoming a figure in the low blaze. A woman, tall and statuesque, covered her mouth in horror as tears streamed from her eyes, and she shook her head in denial, bending as though in physical pain.

Margaret's mother!

Shocked, Ayden blinked, and the image dissolved.

This is the grief of a mother who lost her child.

On the veranda, oil lamps glowed at each of the tables.

Ayden's gaze sought the woman of his vision and found her, seated near the rail.

I should warn her.

A tug on his shirt startled him, and he looked down.

Margaret's dark eyes were wide with unease. "Why did you stand up like that? Are you unwell?"

What if it's Margaret?

He gripped his new friend's shoulders and inhaled deeply to control the panic that beat against his chest. The woman in the fire, Margaret's mother, had on the same dress she wore tonight. Urgency compelled him to speak forcefully, "You've got to be careful tonight, you and your brothers. Something horrible is going to happen."

Across the fire, his mother rose from the haybale, her eyes upon him. "Ayden?"

"I had a vision in the fire," he called to his mother. "I'm not certain what will happen, but it is terrible, and I think it will happen to Margaret or her brothers."

"Rubbish." Chantal James called across the gathering. "Some children need to be at the center of attention, no matter who they frighten."

"I'm not lying."

Leader Brown beat Chantal and his mother around the fire pit. "Can you tell us what you saw?"

"Are you honestly pandering to this child?" Chantal demanded as she approached Ayden and Margaret.

Ayden's mother narrowed her eyes and hurried to stand beside her son. "What did you see?"

"I saw Mrs. James," he told his mother. He glanced at Margaret, and then Chantal. "You were wearing the gown you have on, and you were..." he hesitated, searching for the right words to convey his vision. "You were overcome with grief."

"Garrett, are you just going to stand there and listen to this child spin yarns? Me? Overcome with grief." Chantal sniffed. "I think not."

Ayden turned to Margaret. "I didn't mean to scare you, but what I saw is important. I don't want anything to happen to you or your brothers."

"I know." Margaret smiled at him, then cast a nervous glance at her mother. "It's better to know to be better prepared."

"Ridiculous."

"My son has visions which manifest in fire. It's called pyromancy in case you didn't know." Rachael stood behind her son, hands on his shoulders. "You should listen to Ayden's warning."

"Pyromancy? There hasn't been a pyromancer manifest in a century, and you believe your young son can see the future in the fire?" Chantal took another step forward. "Has anything he predicted proven true?"

A cry from the barn interrupted their conversation.

"Rachael," Lyam called from the open barn door, "Sweetheart, come now. Sully's injured."

Rachael was the first into the barn, followed closely by Garrett and then Chantal. The twins raced behind their mother but stopped at the door.

Ayden sank to the haybale, his head in his hands. "I didn't see enough to stop it. I'm sorry."

"Your father said he was hurt, not dead," Margaret laid a comforting hand on Ayden's shoulder. "It will be all right."

"No." Ayden looked up at Margaret. "I don't think it will."

After several minutes, Garrett and Lyam appeared, carrying Sully on clasped arms.

Perspiration dotted Sully's pale face, and his head lolled to the side and rested on Lyam's shoulder.

"Through the kitchen and down the hall, there's a bedroom on the left," Garrett instructed.

The gathering grew silent as they parted to clear a path for the men to cross the yard to the house.

Ayden, his mother, and the James children followed behind, onto the veranda and inside.

In the bedroom, the men gently lay their burden on the bed.

Sully groaned and opened his eyes. "Chantal?"

Margaret's mother dropped to her knees beside the low bed and took her husband's hand. "I'm here, my dear."

"It wasn't Jack's fault, *or* Lyam's," his hoarse words filled the quiet room. "It was mine—all mine." His unbuttoned shirt showed dark red indentations where Jack's hooves had struck. He struggled to take a breath. "You'll need to perform the ceremony tonight without me."

"That's absurd. There won't be a ceremony, not without you...." Chantal quieted as Sully shook his head.

"The boys need to be in the coven...tested...family. You must stand for them." Panting to get his words out, he tried to take a deep breath and winced. "To pray for me."

"Can't you do anything?" Chantal directed her bitter cry and tear-filled eyes at Rachael. "You're a healer. Help him."

"I'm a midwife. The most I can do is ease his pain," Rachael whispered with regret. "If his injury were on the surface, I could knit the skin and stop the bleeding. But your husband's injuries are deep." Her fingertips touched Sully's injured chest, and a golden glow surrounded her hands.

Immediately, Sully's breathing improved, but his eyes remained closed.

"Let's begin the ceremony now. We can implore the Gods to intervene and help him recover." Garrett gripped Chantal's shoulder.

She nodded and rose, gathering her sons with a look. "The large chest has your new robes. Get changed. I'll be there shortly."

"I'd like to induct you both into the coven as well." Garrett watched the twins exit the room then shifted his gaze to the MacKennas.

"I must stay with Mr. James," Rachael said. "Thank you, but it must be another time."

"I don't have a robe," Lyam admitted.

"You'll wear mine." Sully stared with dull pain-filled eyes at Ayden's father. "I owe you for your work," his voice faded.

"You owe him for a crushed lung, and Goddess knows what else." Chantal whirled from the door and marched toward the bed.

"Not his fault. I told you. I did this." Sully's face scrunched with pain as he struggled to speak. "I walked behind Jack—I knew better."

"Shh," Rachael shot Chantal a stern look as her hand glowed with golden comfort. "She loves you, Sully. Your wife is understandably upset over what's happened."

"Take the robe," Sully insisted. His eyes remained closed.

Lyam looked from Chantal's thin-lipped nod to Garrett. "Thank you. I accept both honors."

After they left, Ayden and Margaret remained in Sully's sick room with Rachael.

Ayden brought his mother a chair from the dining room, and Margaret perched on the end of the bed, her hand on her father's leg.

"Is this what you saw?" Margaret murmured to Ayden.

Ayden caught a look of caution from his mother. He shrugged and lifted Margaret's hand in his. "Not exactly. I saw your mother upset with grief. Which she is." He shook his head as sorrow filled his chest. "I didn't know this would happen to your father."

Margaret wiped a tear. "He'll recover, though, won't he?" Her gaze lifted from her father to Rachael.

"We pray he will."

Margaret looked up at Ayden for confirmation.

"I didn't see what upset your mother, but she's plenty upset right now." He tightened his grip on her hand. "I didn't see the outcome, only the grief."

Margaret nodded. "So, we should pray."

Quiet filled the room. Outside, the day had completed its journey into night. The ceremony began, and the children not old enough to be involved with the coven ritual played tag beneath the torches in the yard.

Ayden's mother, eyes closed, sat with one hand on Sully James's chest. A gentle, steady glow edged her fingers. After some time, her lashes lifted, and she stared into Ayden's eyes with a sad, steady gaze.

She's telling me he's not going to make it.

Margaret's eyes, still clenched in prayer, laid spiky lashes on her pale cheeks.

"Perhaps you two should go outside and get some fresh air."

Margaret nodded and stood—her hands clenched before her. "The meeting will be almost over. We'll see them coming."

Ayden rose as hurried footsteps sounded in the house. Before he and Margaret reached the door, Chantal sailed into the room.

She came to a halt. Her attention focused on the ghastly hue of her husband's face. Her trembling hand covered her mouth in horror as tears streamed from her eyes.

She shook her head in denial and bent at the waist, her arm around her stomach as she trembled in silence. The dark robe slipped from her shoulders and dangled helplessly from her forearms. When she straightened, her chin quivered, and she whispered, "How is he? How's Sully?"

Rachael's voice was clear and soft, her eyes again shut. "He fell into a light sleep ten minutes ago."

"Can he hear me?"

Rachael inhaled. Her chin rose, and her head tipped as though listening to Sully's thoughts. "He knows you're here."

"Sully?" Chantal staggered to the bedside and perched on the mattress. She took her husband's face in her hands. "Darling, can you hear me?"

Ayden's mother's eyes opened. Her urgent gaze pierced him, then slanted toward the door.

Take the girl and go.

"Come on, Margaret." Ayden draped his arm around his new friend and steered her out the door. He led her down the hall, through the kitchen, and to the back door.

Her brothers waited on the veranda. "How is he?" they chimed in unison.

Ayden pushed open the screen door, and Margaret rushed into Bayard's arms, hugging him around the waist. "I don't know. He looks like he's sleeping."

Bayard lifted his gaze to Ayden. "And your mother?"

"She's doing everything she can."

"Your father spoke of what happened during the meeting." Bayard stared evenly into Ayden's eyes. "Before we prayed. He said my father approached Jack from the rear, and although Jack was calm and reassured, his hooves were sore and damaged from the poor trim and shoes. When startled, Jack struck out."

Lyam and Garrett made their way across the yard. A dozen robed members spoke in small groups while tired children leaned in their mothers' arms. A few broke away and headed toward the tents. The carnival atmosphere had gone in the wake of the James tragedy.

Garrett shook several hands then stepped onto the veranda. "Are the women with Sully? How's he doing?" He looked to Ayden.

Ayden shook his head and lowered his eyes.

"Nooo..." the anguished denial stretched into a bitter and broken cry.

Garrett jerked open the screened door and rushed inside.

Lyam followed right after.

"I'll go," Bernard told his brother, and Bayard nodded.

"Let's go to the tent, Mags." Bayard steered Margaret away from the porch and gave Ayden a nod. "I'll take off this robe and tell you about our testing." Sadness colored his voice, along with the determination to keep his sister away from their mother's heartrending cries.

Margaret pulled away and looked back at Ayden. "Thank you for trying to warn us."

Ayden shoved his hands deep into his pockets and nodded. "I wish I'd seen more."

"I know you do. Good night."

Bayard wrapped his arm around the back of her neck, and she hugged her brother's waist as they left the torchlight and continued into the moonlit clearing behind the barn.

Chapter 5

Chantal James

—

"Sully?" The sudden pressure in Chantal's chest forced the air from her lungs and made her heart skip a beat. She rushed to her husband's side and took his face in her hands. "Darling, can you hear me?"

His lashes fluttered open, bit by bit, until he looked into her eyes. He gasped sharply and murmured, "I waited for you."

Her throat swelled closed, and she fought back the tears that stung her eyes. Sully's last image of her shouldn't be a distraught and tear-stained face. A tear slid down her cheek despite her best efforts, and she brushed it away.

Sully can't die. Not so sudden. Not like this!

But he was dying.

The worthless healer grimaced, and the golden light around her hands pressed tight to his chest increased, but there would be no last-minute reprieve.

Sully was about to leave her.

Chantal forced a wavering smile. "I know you waited." Her voice broke, and she pulled a handkerchief from her sleeve and held it beneath her nose. As though the white cloth would staunch the shriek forming inside her head. "I love you, Sully."

His breath, labored and hitched, failed to fill his lungs. His lips were blue. With the final air inside him, he forced the words out. "I love you." His mouth opened again to gasp air, but he could not inhale.

"Do something," Chantal hissed at Rachael.

As though Chantal's bitter grief relieved Rachael of her efforts, the golden glow faded, and she lifted her hands from Sully's damaged chest. "The Goddess has taken him. I am deeply sorry."

The fragile barrier holding Chantal's grief at bay buckled. "No." She shook Sully's shoulders as more tears swelled from her eyes, blocking her vision. "No, no, no." Her head tipped back as she drew a deep, ragged breath, then screamed at Sully, at the Goddess, at her shattered life, "*Noooo!*"

Her hands, like claws, raised in hatred at the fates, and the useless healer, the incompetent farrier, and their pathetic pyromancer child. The sobs rose to screams, out of control and unbalanced.

Then a golden calm descended across her mind.

"Sleep," the healer murmured.

And she did.

When she woke, sunlight filtered into the room around the half-drawn curtains. She lay fully clothed on an old red bedcovering, a crocheted blanket, zigzagging with color covered her dark green dress.

Margaret, her bottom in the chair, her head in her arms on the mattress, slept quietly beside Chantal.

Sully would never let Margaret win at chess again. Never sneak another piece of apple pie for them to share on the back porch. Never watch her fall in love, never—

Chantal firmly closed the door to those thoughts.

If I think of the never mores, I will lose my mind.

Her long-manicured fingers gently brushed her daughter's cheek.

Her face is thinner, more mature.

She brushed Margaret's hair from her cheek.

My baby's gone too.

Tears stung Chantal's eyes.

I certainly won't see Sully home and buried if I keep on with this thinking. Be strong.

"Mama?" Her boys hesitated near the door. "Are you all right?"

Chantal managed a smile as Margaret raised her head and stared at her with sleep-filled eyes. "As right as I can be." She cleared her throat and pushed herself to a sitting position. "What time is it?"

"Almost noon. Leader Brown wanted us to check on you, and if you were awake, ask if you wanted something to eat." Bayard came into the room and set his hands lightly on Margaret's shoulders.

"I should eat." Chantal swung her legs from beneath the blanket. "Where are my shoes?"

"Here." Bernard carried her button-up boots from beside the door and knelt at the bedside to button them.

"I am not going to break, you know." She summoned a smile for her children. "I was terribly upset last night. I'm still heartbroken and saddened beyond words at our loss, but I am well."

"That's good," Bernard said without looking up from his task. "We need you." His eyes, so like Sully's, lifted to hers. "We love you."

"Oh." Whatever she had been going to say was crushed by her throat closing. She reached out and embraced all three of her children. "We will make it through this," she whispered brokenly. "I promise you."

In the kitchen, the dishes and tins of food for the coven dinner had been claimed by their owners and taken away.

Garrett stirred a deep pot of what smelled suspiciously like chicken soup. A loaf of bread cooled on the counter near the window.

"Has everyone gone?" Chantal asked.

"It is good to see you up and around, dear lady." Garrett withdrew a stack of bowls and set them on the kitchen table. "I had more roasted chicken than eggs this morning, but I think this will break your fast nicely." He lifted the pot from the stove and put it in the middle of the heavy oak table. "And yes, most of the coven folk have returned home. There are always a few stragglers, and of course, the MacKennas remain."

She hesitated only slightly as she took her seat. "Of course. Did your farrier find no job prospects with your guests last night?"

"He did." Garrett served soup to Chantal and her children, then filled a bowl for himself with the metal dipper. "I've asked them to stay at the farm and mind the animals until I return."

Chantal sipped her soup and stared across the table at her High Priest. "Where are you going?"

Garrett set his spoon beside his bowl and looked solemnly at the newly widowed mother. "I'm returning to Boston with you. There are tasks—things you'll need help with—a funeral service," his voice trailed off beneath her steady gaze. "But we can discuss this after you break your fast."

She pushed the bowl of soup away. "We'll speak of it now."

"As you wish." Garrett nodded. "While you slept, one of the coven members—a handyman—constructed a coffin for Sully. I presume you wish to bury him near your home."

Chantal dropped her eyes to the soup bowl and struggled to keep her voice even and unemotional. "You presume correctly."

"I intend to return with you to help make the arrangements at whichever cemetery you choose and conduct Sully's burial service." Garrett waited for a response. When he received none, he continued, "Unless you wish otherwise, then of course—"

"No. That will be acceptable. Who...?" Chantal cleared her throat and glanced up at Garrett. "Who made the coffin?"

"Wrigley Johnson. We've had several new members since spring. I don't know if you've had the opportunity to meet him."

She shook her head. "A handyman, you say. From Boston?"

"Yes."

"I would like to make his acquaintance. With Sully gone," her throat tightened, and she swallowed before she could continue, "it would be wise to know someone who can help...."

"You have the coven to help you too, Chantal. There's no need to worry or think further down the road at this moment. I'll go with you to Boston and stay as long as you need."

"Thank you."

I should tell Garrett about The Prophecy.

And immediately behind that thought, Sully's voice, clear and sharp, spoke inside her head, *"Is that the most important thing right now, Chantal?"*

She and Sully had changed covens twice since the night the young woman spoke *The Prophecy*. No one in this group had been there when the girl Chantal hardly knew reached for her hand, spoke the prophetic words, and died.

No, dear heart, but I must warn them eventually, even though Garrett will think me hysterical.

"Speaking of it would be a mistake. You must deal with it alone, my darling, should that damned Prophecy ever happen," again, Sully's voice, skeptical as ever, spoke from beyond the grave into her heart.

I have our sons, my dear, and our daughter. If the worst should happen, I will not stand alone.

Outside, two wagons stood harnessed and ready to depart. Jack waited to pull the first wagon.

Chantal came to a sudden halt and shook her head. "No. Not Jack. I'll not have that horse near us."

Garrett heaved a sigh and stared at Chantal, hands on his hips. "Then how do you propose to get home?"

"She can have one of mine." Lyam crossed the yard wiping his hands on a rag. "I'll take Jack."

At Chantal's nod, Lyam changed direction and returned to the barn.

Without discussion, Bern and Bay clattered down the veranda step and raced to Jack, quickly unbuckling the harness. Bay led Jack by the halter into the barn as Lyam returned with his brown gelding.

Lyam and Bernard strapped the gelding to the shafts, and then Lyam secured the girth strap.

"Give the reins to Bernard," Garrett called. He pulled on his leather gloves and spoke in a softer tone to Chantal. "Your children packed the tent and your trunks while you slept. We should head out if we want to reach your house before dark."

Chantal followed him into the yard.

Bernard held the reins as Bayard steadied her climb onto the seat.

"Your gloves and parasol are beneath the buckboard, Mother," Bay said as Chantal adjusted her skirt. "But I'll be darned if I know where Mags is."

"Bay!" Chantal exclaimed. "Mind your tongue."

Bernard snickered at his brother.

Beside the wagon, Garrett patted Lyam's shoulder. "Should you need anything while I'm gone, take a horse and ride south along the main road."

"We came through the town on our way here. We'll be fine." He held the halter as Garrett climbed onto the seat, then handed him the reins. "You think you'll be in Boston for two weeks, you said?"

Garrett met Chantal's steady gaze and nodded. "Or less."

"Most likely less." Chantal opened her parasol. "But we can't leave without my daughter."

"Ayden?" Lyam called toward the barn.

Ayden and Margaret crossed from the shade of the barn into the sunlight. Ayden looked up and acknowledged his father with a glance, then ducked his head to listen to his companion speak. They stopped for a moment, and Ayden lifted a string of linked clover flowers over her head.

Margaret accepted the gift solemnly, then turned and hurried past Garrett's wagon, which held her father's coffin, to Bayard, who waited beside their wagon.

"You're leaving Jack?" Margaret asked her mother as Bay helped her into the back of the wagon.

"I am," Chantal pointed forward for Bernard to head out. "What did you need to say to the boy that was so important?"

Bayard settled beside his sister as the wagon jerked into motion.

"I told him what to try to manifest different elements."

"How would you know that?" Bay asked.

"I watched you and Bern."

"You told him what we did?" Bern exclaimed.

"You weren't secret about it."

"All right, enough," Chantal scolded. "Has he manifested? Have you?"

"I haven't, but I'll keep trying." Margaret met her mother's gaze with a maturity Chantal found disconcerting. "Ayden manifested *Earth*. I saw him. And, of course, *Fire* with his visions."

"Visions, whether in water, fire, or dreams, is not a manifestation of the elements. It is a gift from the *Spirit*, or the Goddess if you prefer. If that is all he has done with fire, then he hasn't manifested *Fire* at all."

Margaret nodded, looked back at the wagon that followed them, then wiped her cheek with the shirtsleeve she had balled in her fist.

Bayard opened his arms, and her daughter tucked her head against her brother's shoulder.

Chantal shifted her gaze forward and fought her own hopeless sense of loss.

"Be kind to the children. They've lost their father," her husband's tender voice spoke into her heart.

But what of my loss, my love?

No one answered her question, and the road home stretched out before her.

Hours later, as they rounded Parker Hill, Chantal touched Bernard's shoulder. "Pull to the side. I need to speak to Garrett."

Bernard slowed the gelding to a stop and waved the priest forward.

"Is something amiss?" Garrett reined in beside Bernard.

Chantal leaned forward. "I've given Sully's resting place some thought. There are three or four burying grounds in Boston. I like both Granary and Central, although I think Central will be more accommodating to our needs. Besides, Sully's brother is buried there. Do you know of it?"

"I do. Central is on the south side of the Common, off Boylston, between Charles and Tremont." Garrett lifted his flat-top straw hat and brushed the sweat from his brow with his shirtsleeve. His jacket lay folded on the seat beside him, shed, no doubt, as the heat of the day assailed him.

"Yes. If you would, please go there directly and speak to the caretaker. Tell him to open a grave in the James family plot for tomorrow." Chantal pulled a handkerchief from her sleeve and covered her nose and mouth. "Preferably, the one beside his brother, Samuel. The sooner, the better."

"I can do that."

She pulled a calling card from her handbag and passed it to Bernard. "Our address. You'll stay with us while in town. I insist."

Garrett had opened his mouth to protest but shut it with a small smile. "Thank you."

"Take us home," she directed Bernard, and the wagon moved forward.

With the children safely tucked into their beds, Chantal accepted a cup of tea from her housemaid, took a quick sip, then added sugar.

At a nod from Chantal, the maid disappeared from the kitchen, leaving Chantal alone at the servant's table.

She couldn't bear the dining room tonight. Not yet. Not when she and Sully had spent evenings alone there for years, sipping tea, and talking, once the children were abed.

A soft tap at the back door drew her from her memory. With a sigh, she rose from the table and cracked open the door.

Garrett stood on the back step. His hands shoved deep into his pockets. "All the lights are out except for the kitchen. I didn't want to wake the household, so I tried the back door. I didn't expect the lady of the house to answer."

Chantal pushed open the door.

Garrett came inside and closed the kitchen door behind him.

"The water in the kettle is hot if you'd like some tea." Chantal took her seat.

"No, thank you." Garrett settled into the chair across from Chantal. "Everything is arranged at the Central Burying Ground. The gravedigger will bury the casket beside Sully's brother tonight."

Chantal nodded but didn't look up from her tea.

"We will say our prayers and give Sully our final goodbye over his closed grave in the morning."

Grief washed over Chantal, and she lifted a trembling hand to her mouth. Unable to utter a sound without allowing a sob to escape, she nodded her understanding.

Garrett waited until Chantal composed herself.

After a few moments, she raised her tear-filled gaze to meet his. "I understand." She pulled her handkerchief from her sleeve, touched the corner of both eyes, then lifted her teacup with a steady hand.

"I've no wish to bother you, and it has been a very long day for us both." Garrett rose to his feet.

"Yes. Of course." Chantal set her cup into its dish. "Through the dining room is the stairs. The open door along the upper hallway will be the guest room. You should have fresh linen and water waiting for you. I will retire once I've finished my tea."

"Then I'll say goodnight, Chantal." He paused before he entered the dining room and looked back, meeting her gaze. "Let me say one last time how sorry I am for the loss of Sully. By the Goddess, a better man never walked this earth."

Chantal nodded, dabbed her nose with her handkerchief. "Thank you, Garrett. Good night."

She listened to his footsteps climb the stairs then traverse the hallway above her. When silence settled again in the house, she finished her tea.

The full moon set the drawn curtains aglow as she made her way to her room.

Our room.

She undressed in the darkness, refusing to wake the maid to assist her. On their late evenings, Sully acted as her lady's maid, but never again.

I must learn to take care of myself.

Beneath the covers, she turned her face to Sully's pillow and cried until sleep overcame her.

A thick cool fog rolled inland the following day, settling like a silent shroud over the quiet graveyard.

She buried Sully near the western edge of the Central Burying Ground, beside his twin brother. The park setting provided a quiet resting place for Chantal's beloved husband, not far from the Public Gardens across Charles Street. Sully and Sam were together again.

Sully would like that.

Garrett and Chantal wore their fine coven robes. The priest and the widow, accompanied by the three children, were the only mourners at the short service.

"*Lord and Lady,*

"*Be with us as we call upon your daughter, Hecate,*

"Goddess of the Underworld and

"Mighty Queen of the Night.

✳

"We beseech you, Divine Light,

"To lift your torch and guide this loved one,

"Sullivan James,

"Upon his journey to your realm.

✳

"Mother of all,

"Offer us comfort in our time of grief.

"And remind us that all that pass from life shall be reborn.

✳

"Mistress of Magic,

"Who stands between life and death,

"Hear our prayer,

"And welcome this departed soul."

Garrett's prayer continued, but Chantal stopped listening, her attention turned inward. Sully's voice, distant and soft in her mind, had stopped speaking, yet she strained to hear it.

On her left, Margaret sniffed.

Bayard tightened his arm around his sister's shoulder.

To Chantal's right, Bernard stood quietly composed, a bulwark against the fog. Sad but balanced. Resigned. Resolute.

Who knows what kind of exchange is going on between their minds—twyned together—never alone?

Chantal's isolation clawed up her throat, nearly choking her.

Sully no longer spoke to her heart. The veil between them, once thin, ethereal, and unreal, had become hard and final.

Hecate has taken him away. I have no choice but to let him go.

She fought back a sob and pressed her handkerchief to the corner of each eye before tears could fall.

She raised her head as the silence stretched around her.

"Mama?" Margaret tugged her robe.

Garrett's sharp glance pierced the fog, his gaze locked with hers in immediate understanding.

"Let's give your mother a moment." He shepherded her children toward the graveyard entrance. "We'll wait for you at the carriage."

Chantal nodded. Eyes closed, she listened to their footfalls fade. When silence surrounded her, she inhaled the damp morning mist and expanded her senses. The air was full of moisture as the earth longed for the sun's warmth. Her spirit, chained to her body, yearned to soar and find Sully's essence in the mist. Instead, her senses discovered only a nest of birds, tricked by the low clouds, beginning to stir nearby.

"The Goddess damn you, Sully, for leaving me here without you." Her ungloved hands crushed the cuttings she clutched to her chest: the flowering plant, a gift from Sam James years ago.

Her heart empty and her mind blank, she stared at Sam's headstone.

From the corner of her eye, a flicker of light darting through the graveyard caught her attention. Brighter than a firefly, the steady spark approached her brother-in-law's headstone, then paused, bobbing up and down, its glow magnified by the mist.

"Well, hello there, little one."

She knew of fairies, of course, but she'd never seen one. The shy magical creatures were rarer than hen's teeth. That one would approach her in a graveyard of all places was astounding.

Another bright spark of light flashed past her head.

She spun to watch its progress.

It meandered for several seconds, then floated back to the first spark which hung in the air over Sam's grave.

"Are you twins then? If you've come to lift my spirits, you have certainly succeeded."

If they communicated at all, it was only with each other.

Like every set of twins I've ever known—the two that have passed and the two waiting for me at the carriage.

She bent to place the flowers on the graves, splitting the floral cuttings evenly between the brothers. Finally, she knelt in the damp dirt beside Sully's grave and rested her hand on the soil.

Be at peace, my love. I pray the Goddess holds you and Sam in her heart. Rest easy, dear one. Know that I will care for your children to the end of my days. I will give my life for theirs if needs be.

When she opened her eyes, the sprites were gone. She rose to her feet and brushed the soil from her skirt, then followed the path to the exit and her children.

Chapter 6

Ayden MacKenna

—

October 19, 1842 – The Brown Farm

The length of his father's old hooded robe was only a bit long. At fourteen and a half years old, Ayden almost matched Lyam's six-foot, two-inch height. However, the sleeves hung past his hands—a testament to the width of the previous owner's mature shoulders.

Ayden jumped from the back of their wagon and ran to the end of the apprentice line entering Brown's large ceremonial barn. He yanked the hood over his head and crossed his arms like his brethren, tucking his hands inside the sleeves, then followed a young woman inside. Nerves tingled along his scalp in anticipation of the magical test to come.

Inside, bone-dry dirt stirred with each step as the candidates circled the elders and lined up against the wall. There were eleven candidates in all.

Ayden fought the urge to rub the irritating particles from his nose.

The prayers had ended before the young applicants entered. Those who did not wish to witness the testing took their leave to join their friends and family outside. The coven members who remained faced the line of young candidates.

Ayden's parents slipped into the large barn, robed and silent, and paced across the back to the far side.

An emergency had kept his father at work longer today than planned. The delay resulted in his parents' absence from the earlier prayer meeting and Ayden almost missing the test and induction ceremony.

Ayden had never been inside the ceremonial barn until tonight.

On the ground, in the middle of the structure, the black pentacle etched into the dirt floor shimmered like polished obsidian. In the center of the sacred star burned a small fire. Smoke lifted from the wood, disturbed by the movement inside the room, adding to the irritants which tickled Ayden's nose.

Leader Brown nodded to the congregation then turned to the line of young witches. "Welcome applicants. Thank you for your patience. I know everyone is anxious to get back out beneath the light of this beautiful Hunter's moon and celebrate. As we have a record number of candidates tonight, I shall attempt to be as brief and efficient as possible.

"Each one of you is here on a recommendation from one of our members." He gestured to the small crowd. "Should you prove proficient with the elements tonight, and join this coven as a member, your sponsor or family member, will be responsible for your behavior with regards to our coven rules, including that of your discretion. We are happy you have decided to join us.

"Tonight, we will assess your abilities and celebrate your most persuasive skills. As you know, all witches can manipulate each of the four elements to some degree. However, it is normal for only one or two facets to respond to your will with any significance.

"I suspect you already know which spirits grant you their particular favor. Therefore tonight, we determine your superior and secondary skills. We will then welcome you into our congregation as part of our Samhain celebration on the thirty-first.

"Let us begin."

Gordon Carmichael, the first in line, pushed back his hood and stepped forward.

Leader Brown shook his hand. "Turn around, Mr. Carmichael, and face your friends."

Gordon pivoted. With an arrogant smirk, he pinned his gaze on his chum, Milton, who waited next in line.

He spoke to Gordon but included everyone in the explanation. "You will be given several small tasks. How well you perform these will show us the extent of your skills with each element.

"Are you ready, Mr. Carmichael?"

"I am."

"Good. We begin, as always, to the east, with the *element of air*."

Gordon's cocky grin faltered, and he swallowed.

"Existing all around us, Air is one of the most difficult elements to manipulate."

Chuckles and nods of agreement rippled through the watching coven members.

"Mr. Carmichael, if you would, please exhale a breath and blow the hoods back from your compatriots along the wall."

Gordon took a deep breath and blew outward between pursed lips.

Milton chuckled as his cowl slipped from his head.

"All of the hoods, Mr. Carmichael," Leader Brown said.

Gordon blew out another breath, his round face red and strained. Spittle flew as he expelled his breath harder, but the headcovers remained in place.

"Let's move to the south and the *element of fire*."

Gordon huffed in frustration as he gulped air, then nodded. His smug grin returned.

"Please call a candle-sized flame to your right hand."

Gordon lifted his palm, and a spark flew from the central fire and danced above his hand.

"Now pass that element to your left hand and call another to your right. Keep both flames the same size and separate."

Gordon's brows twitched as he moved the flame to his left hand.

"You can do it," Milton whispered.

A moment later, a flicker blossomed above Gordon's right hand. Its light glistened in the sweat on Gordon's face.

"Extinguish both flames, Mr. Carmichael. Well done. You show a predisposition for *Fire*."

Murmured conversation filtered around the spectators.

"Now, Mr. Carmichael, we look to the west and the *element of water*." Brown indicated a bucket on the floor close to the central fire. "Please call a small globe from our source to your right hand."

Water sloshed from the bucket, dampening the dirt nearby, but Gordon's hand remained empty.

Leader Brown watched the water for several seconds then faced the candidates. "Now we reach to the north—"

"Wait. I can do this," Gordon interrupted. He ground his clenched teeth while perspiration slicked his face.

"You have touched the water, young man, but it does not respond to your call. Let us continue, or we will miss the festivities." Brown turned his back to Gordon and paced away as the water bucket continued to splash. He waited a moment, then turned and sauntered back to the applicants.

"North represents the *earth-elements*. Please cease attempting to call water, Mr. Carmichael. Call a stone or a pinch of dirt to your right hand instead."

Gordon shot a look of angry frustration over his shoulder at Brown, and the water stilled. A small stone near Ayden's foot rose into the air and levitated to Gordon's hand.

"Pass it to your left and call another, as you did with *Fire*."

A pebble beside Leader Brown's foot rose then fell back to the dirt. Dust rippled between Gordon and Milton, but Gordon's hand remained empty.

"Thank you, Mr. Carmichael. Your principal element is *Fire*, and your secondary is *Earth*." Brown extended his arm to the audience. "You may stay and watch your friends or join the festivities outside."

Gordon gave Leader Brown a brief nod, jerked up his hood over his tall brow, and shouldered his way through the small group of onlookers. A group of adults near the applicants followed the young man outside.

As a midwife, Ayden's mother used the same elements Gordon could manipulate, *Fire* and *Earth*, to assist during birth. His mother's skills were not strong enough to bestow the rare title of Healer, although she claimed that knowledge of internal organs had more to do with her limitations than skill strength.

I wouldn't want Gordon to heal me.

At the head of the line, Milton took Gordon's place, and each applicant stepped forward.

Leader Brown moved swiftly through the elements, dispensing with previously voiced explanations, and proclaimed Milton's strengths were *Earth* and *Air*.

Finally, Ayden's turn came to step forward. He lowered his hood and turned his back to the coven leader.

The large barn had emptied of spectators. Ayden's mother and father stood near the firepit, the only people in the ample open space.

"Good morning, Mr. MacKenna. Since there are no longer compatriots behind you, please use the *air element* to push back several of our members' hoods." Brown chuckled as he realized there were only four of them in the barn. "The hoods of your parents, then."

Ayden locked eyes with his father ten feet away and inhaled, saying a quick prayer to the Goddess. He blew the air from his lungs, intending to unseat only his father's cowl. His mother smiled with delight as her hood flew back from her head as well.

"Very good. Now call *Fire*."

Ayden lifted his hand, and a tiny flame flew from the central fire. He passed it to his left hand and held two.

"*Air* and *Fire*, a good combination—" Garrett halted and stared at the globe of water rotating above Ayden's right hand. "You manipulate *Water* too? How strong are you?"

Without pause, Ayden transferred the water to his left hand and called another.

"*Earth*?" Leader Brown gazed steadily at Ayden; eyes narrowed.

Ayden lifted both hands. Dirt and small stones rose from the ground as though awaiting Ayden's desire. Two stones from either side of the structure sailed over his parent's heads and hovered above Ayden's hands.

Leader Brown chuckled. "Your skills are remarkable. To be equally strong in all four elements makes you something of a prodigy, son."

Ayden released the stones to the ground and turned to the coven leader.

Brown grinned and shook his head with evident delight. "Your numerous abilities are quite a surprise. Can you manipulate more than one element at a time?"

Ayden shrugged. "I don't know, sir. I've never tried."

"Please." Leader Brown crossed to stand beside his parents. "Show us what you can do."

Ayden exhaled slowly then lifted his hands.

In an instant, a small flame danced above his left hand. Over his right, a large droplet of water spun an inch from his palm. He extended his right arm and lifted the water higher and then bid it remain there. A nervous flutter tickled his stomach as he reached out to *Earth*. His eyelids closed to sense each of the elements better. With a flick of his wrist, he drew together a handful of dirt.

The three elements held.

Fire above his left hand, *Earth* in his right, with *Water* suspended above.

He inhaled, then pursed his lips and blew a gentle, steady stream of *Air*—the final element. He bid tiny particles of dust from the dirt glide and dance on the air, encircling each wrist and then around the water above his head. The dust glittered in the firelight.

Three elements, held in a trinity and linked by the fourth, were bound to the will of one man.

Ayden's eyes opened, and he gazed at his work. His brain buzzed with concentration and control. Each element demanded minute adjustment and attention. He had none to spare to gauge his parents or Leader Brown's reaction.

"Astounding."

Brown's softly spoken word broke Ayden's concentration, and his control collapsed. The tiny flame extinguished. He jumped back as the water struck the ground. He tossed the handful of dirt on top of the moisture then turned to stare at the leader. "This isn't normal?"

"No, son, no!" Brown exclaimed with excitement. "I'd have thought *Fire* would be your preeminent skill, what with your ability in pyromancy, but to be able to manipulate all of the elements equally, and at the same time, well son—I've never seen the like."

"We don't want anyone to know," Lyam stated firmly.

Leader Brown's enthusiasm stilled. His animation and excitement suspended as he turned to the parents. "Your son's abilities are remarkable," Brown insisted. "A thing to be proud of."

"I am proud of my son." Lyam crossed the short distance and gripped his son's shoulder. "However, some members already hold his unique pyromancy ability against him. Declaring him an elemental prodigy would add insult to injury in their eyes."

"You speak of Chantal James." Brown rubbed his face as he considered Lyam's request. "I agree. She can be a hard woman. The loss of Sully weighs on her soul. But I didn't realize she fostered resentment toward Ayden."

"She harbors it towards our family," Rachael said. "No one knows of my son's exceptional skills except us." She turned her gaze to her son. "Pick your two strongest skills."

Ayden shrugged. "I don't think I can. There isn't a stronger one."

"Proclaim *Fire* his prominent ability." Lyam took Rachael's hand, shifting his gaze between Ayden and Leader Brown. "Make *Water* his secondary."

"That's a weak combination." Garrett narrowed his eyes at Lyam.

"But that's what we want," Ayden spoke, drawing his elder's attention. "Don't you see? I'm already too much of a distraction."

"If that's your wish. I'll agree, but on one condition." Garrett's stern voice belied the twinkle in his eye. "Allow Ayden to stay with me until the Samhain gathering. I want to work with him and test the extent of his power. What's more, I could use his help setting up the festivity games."

***

Garrett dusted his felt hat against his slacks as they watched the last wagon pull out of the yard. "Most will be back in under a fortnight for Samhain."

He pulled the hat over his receding hairline and walked across the wide front clearing to the farm road.

Ayden followed the coven leader down the dirt drive that rounded the house and led to the working barn.

"On this side—" Garrett pointed at the eight-foot-tall, dry leafy stalks beside the road. "We'll need to flatten enough to make a corn maze in the field." He paused, hands on his narrow hips. "Your *earth-skill* will be helpful for this. We'll draw up a maze plan tonight. We can put a cushioned stool in the center. The ladies will like that."

Garrett continued to the back of the house. "The long tables will set close to the porch, on this side of the firepit. Over there, by the barn, we'll put a greased pig corral." He laughed. "Those are rare fun for the younger children, and Fat Sal has six piglets old enough not to be injured in the ruckus.

"Just down from the pigs, will be barrels with water and apples. The womenfolk will think it too messy, but the boys and men enjoy it." He strode past the covered porch toward the meeting barn. "In this area, we'll have musicians." He grinned at Ayden. "We have several members with musical skills. There is a game played with chairs and music. When the music stops, whoever cannot find a seat is eliminated. Everyone likes that game."

"And of course, we'll have the bonfire in the center of the yard. After sunset, those who wish can congregate in the large barn and attempt to contact the dead."

"Can they do that?" Ayden stared at the meeting barn.

"Talk to the dead?" Garrett lifted his hat and scratched his head. "Some swear they can, but I'm not the one to ask. It takes a spiritual skill I don't have." He settled his hat. "They tell me it's easier to reach across the void the closer you get to Samhain."

Their stroll continued around the house and stopped beside the front porch. "We'll give our thanks to the Lord and Lady for a bountiful harvest and pray for a prosperous new year around the bonfire. Then, after our prayers, we'll welcome the new members."

"What do the new members do?"

"Step forward when your name is called. Accept the designation of your elements. For you, *Fire* and *Water*."

Ayden's eyebrows rose. "But we will work on *Earth* and *Air* while I'm here."

"Ha! Even so. We shall work on them all." He picked up a stone from the yard, tossing it in the air and catching it. "Catch this." Garrett drew back his arm and threw the rock down the drive. It sailed twenty feet through the air before it fell to the ground and rolled to a stop. He turned to Ayden. "You were supposed to catch and hold it."

"Catch it? You mean stop it in the air?"

Garrett exhaled with annoyance and narrowed his eyes at Ayden. "Yes. What did you think I meant?"

Ayden nodded and squared his stance. "Try it again."

As the fist-sized stone flew from Garrett's hand, Ayden's eyelids fluttered closed, and his hand rose. *Earth-power* reached across the distance and took control of the rock, stopped its flight, and held it motionless in the air. Ayden opened his eyes.

Another projectile flew from Garrett's hand, then another. When the leader stopped throwing, seven stones of diverse sizes hung motionless above the drive.

"Now, hold them as they are, and call a flame." Garrett shook his finger at Ayden. "Not draw it to you, mind, but to those rocks, you hold in the air. And don't drag the flame from here to there—capture it, contain it—and make it appear out there." Garrett's pointed at the seven rocks floating in the air.

"Where's the fire?"

"Where?"

"There's no fire out here."

"Ah. Well. As for that, I happen to know there is fire within your reach, but you'll need to find it yourself. Search with your senses, but remember, do not drag the spark across the distance. Find it. Control it. Then have it appear within your ornamental rock hanging." Garrett chuckled.

Ayden swallowed, took a breath, and lowered his chin. As his inner perception reached out, his eyes closed. His awareness circled the front yard then extended outward in a widening sphere, drawn in two directions—toward the stoked embers of the fireplace inside and the sudden flare of a matchstick along the farm road.

"Someone's coming." His eyes opened in time to see his carefully held stones strike the dirt. In moments, the sound of horses' hooves and the jingle of tack echoed in the autumn silence.

Garrett mounted the steps of the porch and studied a trail of dust that hung low over the road beyond the trees. "What do you think? Members returning or strangers?"

Ayden's gaze returned to the dirt drive, and he reached out with *earth-sense* as he hadn't done since his encounter with the wolves so long ago.

Four horses, tired and thirsty. Each carried the weight of a rider. Three dogs loped along at their side.

"Four strangers. The horses have been ridden hard. They have dogs."

Their movement appeared beyond the leafless trees before they rounded the bend in the road. Three thin men rode, weary in the saddle.

Three?

"There are three men then," Ayden muttered.

"You thought there were four?"

"I did, but there's something—wrong." Ayden swallowed and wiped damp palms against his trousers. "Their animals need water." His senses still queried the approaching strangers.

"I'll talk with them here as long as I can, then take them around to the well pump trough." Garrett came down the stairs. "I need you to head to the big barn. Make sure the pentacle is covered."

"The big pentacle on the floor?"

"Yes, of course. Spread tack and tools from the working barn on the ground in the big barn or toss hay across it. Move the horses to the big barn. I want it to be unappealing. If they insist on hospitality for tonight, I want them in the small barn." He gave Ayden's shoulder a nudge. "Now go."

Ayden blinked as his wandering senses returned. He gave Garrett a brief nod and raced around the house to the large barn.

He yanked the metal pin from the simple latch and pulled the door open. Inside, late afternoon light filtered by the slats across the smoke hole in the ceiling laid bright stripes across the west wall. On the dirt, in the center of the room, the large five-pointed star within a circle glittered, each stroke etched in smooth black stone four inches wide. The pentacle covered over half of the floor and shone brilliantly even in the dim light.

Ayden hesitated. The use of magic at home was frowned upon and sometimes downright forbidden. They weren't that far in distance or time from Salem and lived in a busy city. Still, this situation called for the use of his elemental magic.

Garrett's hearty, "Hello," echoed around the side of the house.

Ayden lifted his hands.

Earth.

The hard-packed dirt rippled and appeared to liquify around the obsidian design. Ayden gave a grunt as he forced his will upon the dry ground and pushed at the air with his hands. Dirt shifted and swirled over the black stone circle, and five-pointed star then settled. When the pentacle lay hidden beneath the soil, he pushed his hands down, repacking the ground solid.

The entire task might have taken ten minutes or an hour. Ayden's concentration was so deep, he'd lost track of time.

His gaze searched the floor of the barn for any mistake in his work. Satisfied the sacred circle lay well-hidden, he hurried outside into the afternoon sunlight.

Voices carried from the far side of the house. "Is it just you on this big farm?"

"Middlin' size farm, and I have men who work for me." Garrett sauntered into view, glanced at Ayden, then turned his attention back to the new guests. "There's water for your mounts." He pointed to the trough.

Two men led their horses around the house while the third trudged behind the others, the youngest by his size. He led two mares, one with a body tied across the animal's back.

They looked like brothers, all cut from the same dusty bolt of cloth, as Ayden's mother would have said, with the same hawkish nose, lean frame, and the same color hair.

Their dogs, three big bloodhounds, rose on hind legs to reach the trough and lapped eagerly.

"What's in your barns?" The deeply tanned man with tangled, shoulder-length white hair stepped forward. A worn felt hat covered the crown of his head. He dropped the reins as his mare found the trough.

"Animals. Equipment. A couple wagons. Hay, corn, and beans after harvest 'til it's sold." Garrett hooked his thumbs in his belt and smiled at the men.

"Anything in there now?" All four horses had found the water.

Garrett shrugged. "Crops are gone from the big 'un. Just some winter hay." He indicated the large barn and then thumbed over his shoulder at the other. "The working barn is being cleaned." He lifted his chin and voice toward Ayden. "Tired already?"

"No, sir." Ayden ducked his chin and continued to the smaller building.

"We'll inspect both barns and search inside the house."

"Inspect? Search?" Garrett crossed his arms, his voice tightened. "Under whose authority and for what purpose?"

The tone of Garrett's voice halted Ayden in his tracks, and he watched the group around the water trough.

The middle brother, by height, pulled a long rifle from his saddle and tucked his jacket behind the gun on his hip. "Under the authority of *Who the hell's gonna stop us?*" He grinned and spit. "And since ya asked, we're looking for run-aways. We know you Northerners like helping slaves hide from their proper owners. We have a bounty for three—and we only need two more before we start home." He tipped his head to the body tied over the fourth horse. "They take 'em back dead or alive."

"Easy now, Clifford." The first brother chuckled and whipped his sleeve beneath his nose. "Farmer Brown won't give us no trouble. He's a smart man."

"You're slave catchers." Garrett raised his hands and took a step back. "You'll find no run-aways here."

"I ain't seen your womenfolk." Clifford stalked up to Garrett, holding his long rifle. "Where's your wife? Your daughter? Get them out here."

"Enough, Cliff. If they're here, we'll find 'em." He snapped his fingers at the youngest man. "Inspect the barns."

The young slave catcher hurried around the end of the trough as he eyed Ayden.

"Take your weapon, Clyde." Exasperation bled from the leader's voice. "Dumb-ass."

"Oh yeah!" Clyde reversed course back to the horses. He pulled a small handgun from his bag. "Thank ya for the reminder, Clem." Then scurried toward Ayden, brandishing the weapon. "Open up."

"Ayden," Garrett called. "Open the barn for Mr. Finley, then come wait with me." The coven leader's voice held a note of warning.

Ayden unlatched the barn and let the door swing wide. Once the white-haired Clyde passed into the semi-darkness of the working barn, Ayden ground his teeth and crossed the yard. He halted beside the trough—hands pushed deep into his pockets.

"Cliff, search the house," Clem instructed the middle brother, then worked the pump handle, and water fell into the trough.

Elemental magic called for Ayden to do something. The *Water* whispered as it fell into the slender water canal—*Fire* banked inside the stove in the house beckoned—primal *Earth* and *Air* around him, begged—*do something, we are with you.*

"Garrett?" Ayden clenched his teeth as Clem Finley drenched his handkerchief in the water and washed his face.

"No." Garrett's faint voice carried the force of a command. Their eyes met, and the leader's alert blue eyes held him. "They will leave us unmolested. And we will let them."

Clem chuckled and looked across the water. "Yeah, you will."

The middle brother stomped onto the porch and threw open the back door. "Hello?" he hollered. Inside, dishes crashed. The sound splintered inside Ayden's head like shards of glass.

Garrett's warm hand gripped his forearm. "Bide, son."

"Nothin' in here, Clem," the youngest Finley called. He captured his old felt hat before it slid from his head and hastened to the big barn. "'Sept horses, pigs, tack, and an old wagon."

Doors slammed inside the farmhouse.

The dogs lost interest in the water and sniffed the ground, circling the horses in ever-widening circles.

"Find anything?" Clem called to the younger brother.

Clyde shook his head and grabbed at his hat as it slid to the side. "Biggest empty barn I've ever seen."

Cliff slammed out of the door with an old burlap sack in his hand. He paused to hitch up his trousers. "There's no one in the house, no dresses in the closets. No women things at all. He has a whole room filled with books." Holding the sack high, he clumped down the short set of steps. "There was a lot of food in the kitchen, so I helped myself." He tied the sack to his saddlebag then narrowed his eyes at Garrett. "Why was there so much food for just you two?"

"We had company this week. You may have passed some of them on the road as you came north."

Clifford nodded. "Yup. A few." He filled his water jug, then mounted his beast. "Much obliged for your hospitality, farmer Brown." He tugged the brim of his old hat and urged his horse forward.

"Never seen a farm with no women." Clem slapped the cork in his water-skin and stowed it in his bag. He fit the toe of his boot in the stirrup then slung his leg over the saddle. "You both take care." He jerked the reins.

Clyde checked the lead to the extra horse, then tightened the rope beneath the horse that held the body. He averted nervous eyes as he mounted, then thundered after his brothers.

"Do you think they'll be back?" Ayden followed Garrett to the front of the house as they both watched the slave catchers depart.

"Hard to say." Garrett spit on the ground, his previously blank face now filled with disgust. "I hope not."

"Then—why didn't we take a stand against them?"

"We use magic against others in defense only. They were no danger to us." Garrett stared into the distance toward the dust hanging over the road. "Besides, those were three vastly different men, each with their own reasons for performing their foul service. Slavery is an ugly business. Hunting escaped men, killing them for a bounty, is just as bad." He shook his head. "The youngest was no more than a child and only doing as he was told."

"How do you know that, and why would their reasons matter?"

"Maybe they don't." Garrett cocked one eyebrow at Ayden. "I also didn't relish the thought of you getting hurt." He shrugged and clapped his hand on Ayden's shoulder. "I would never be able to face your mother." The coven leader mounted the steps to the front porch and opened the door. "Best clean up the mess Clem left for us inside, then we'll get down to the business of planning for Samhain."

Chapter 7

Margaret James

—

October 31, 1842 – The Brown Farm

Their wagon pulled to a halt at the Brown farm under a magnificent blue October sky. Far to the west, Margaret eyed a bank of dark clouds crouched along the horizon. The storm had ceased to advance during the long ride from Boston. Perhaps it would move to the south and miss them altogether.

She gripped Bayard's forearm as he helped her down from the wagon seat, then straightened her short jacket and shook out her skirt. "It seems like forever since I've been here."

Children played near the dried cornfield beside a sign that proclaimed there was a 'Maze Entrance' nearby.

"Not much has changed." Bayard glanced at his brother, who exchanged words with their mother on the far side of the wagon. Slowly his interest returned to his sister. "That's right. You haven't been back since—"

"Since Father died."

Bay lowered his voice. "Do you know why she decided to come today?" His gaze flickered to their mother.

"No." Margaret shook her head, then shrugged. "Samhain, I suppose."

"She didn't come last year," Bay noted.

"Perhaps it was too soon. None of us had a desire to celebrate last year."

"I doubt she's here to celebrate this year either."

"Bay." Bernard waved his hand toward the farmhouse and walked in that direction without looking back.

"Do you always come when he calls?" Margaret queried.

"No, but don't tell him that," Bayard quipped, then rounded the wagon. He called back to her over his shoulder, "See you at supper if it doesn't rain first." He ran to catch up with his twin. In step, they rounded the house toward the working barn.

Chantal had reached the steps of the wraparound porch. She held the bell of her skirt with one hand as she mounted the wide tread, her spine ramrod straight. Her hair had turned ash white over the last year, blending the single lock of white in with the rest. She carried a timeless look, both ancient and youthful.

Mother scares me sometimes.

Left to her own devices, Margaret followed her brothers. Not that she wanted to spend time with them, but they might lead her to another young man—one who had occupied her thoughts with alarming regularity over the last year.

Ayden MacKenna.

Margaret tugged at the waist of the tight-fitting stays worn beneath her dress and jacket. After her menses began last summer, her breasts blossomed, and Mother decided it the proper time for her to wear a woman's long-waisted bodice and floor-length gowns.

While other girls close to her age played with dolls near the dried corn rows, Margaret opened her lace-trimmed parasol and searched for a specific boy whom she could not chase from her mind.

Bay had teased her all summer about her infatuation with their neighbor, Robert Prescott. In one sense, it was true. Rob had been her best friend forever. She confided everything to him.

All except two things.

She never spoke of her family's skill in *elemental magic*, nor her confused feelings for Ayden MacKenna.

Instead, they often spoke of Rob's dream to venture out to sea with his father and his hope to captain a ship of his own one day.

However, since the day she first met Ayden MacKenna, he was the one who held out his hand to her in her dreams.

I wonder how much he's changed since that horrible night.

She waved at her friends as she passed their play circle.

They dissolved into giggles over their dolls while they eyed her outfit and whispered.

Margaret tossed her head and continued past the cornrow maze and around the farmhouse.

In the backyard, long tables stood ready for the mid-day feast. Further on, between the large barns, a split rail enclosure housed the greased piglet game.

Margaret's steps faltered.

Inside the pen, cheering on one of the muddied children, stood Ayden MacKenna. He threw back his head and laughed as the red-faced youngster lost his grip on the squirming animal and fell face-first into the mud.

"You almost had him. Keep trying." His legs, covered in tan-colored trousers, pushed into tall mud-covered boots. Without jacket or vest, his white shirt gaped open as he leaned against the enclosure's rail. "There you go!" He clapped when the muddied child lifted the squealing piglet in the air.

A discussion ensued between the child and Ayden. It ended when the piglet was set free, and the youngster received a candied apple from one of the young women waiting with treats outside the pen.

The girl's gaze lingered on Ayden's open shirt as she leaned to the side and whispered to her dark-haired companion. Both girls dissolved into giggles that hushed when Ayden turned to seek what amused them.

Ayden had matured much more than Margaret could ever have imagined. Too long away from the coven, he was no longer the little boy she remembered.

What if he doesn't recall who I am?

How foolish would she appear if she rushed to him with an enthusiastic greeting only to have him ask her name?

Embarrassed by her excitement at seeing him, she strolled past the greased pig challenge, shielded by both her bonnet and her parasol, and paused at the apple bobbing game.

Watching wet-faced children capture apples with their teeth from a water barrel did not hold her attention for long.

Her jaw clenched at a shrill giggle behind her. Then she spun as the merriment turned into a startled shriek.

A greasy piglet brushed past her skirt and into a group of women watching the apple bobbing. Shrieks and laughter ensued as the ladies ran from the small porker, who turned curly tail and disappeared into the yellowed cornfield.

Next to the pig enclosure, one of the young women helped the other to her feet beside the open gate of the empty pen.

Ayden grabbed at a mud-covered piglet, which squirmed and kicked its way free with a squeal. "Damn!" He leveled an aggravated glare at the two girls. "Why did you open the gate?"

Children laughed and chased a muddy piglet that ran beneath the long tables.

The two young women clung to each other, laughing, as the last piglet escaped around their skirts and into the field beyond.

Ayden shook his head, fists balled on his hips. The once white shirt muddied as well as his chest. "I don't find any of this amusing."

His comment sent the ladies by the pen into another round of hilarity, and even Margaret smiled.

Ayden brushed past the giggling girls and stalked into the cornfield.

"Good luck!" one of the girls called, bringing more laughter from her friend. Arm in arm, they made their way through the long tables to the back porch.

The children lost interest in the empty pig stall and raced to the apple bobbing area.

Margaret stepped away from the crowd and closed her parasol.

Was no one going to help Ayden catch the piglets?

She knew nothing of pigs or how to catch one. She glanced around the gathering for Bayard but didn't find either twin to advise her on pig stalking.

Before she lost her nerve, she untied her bonnet, dropped it and the umbrella near the edge of the field, and hurried into the dried cornfield.

***

Ayden MacKenna

—

Ayden pushed his way through the corn forging a path, ignoring the orderly rows. Anger and annoyance bled together, and he growled deep in his throat and clenched his teeth.

What were those scatterbrain girls thinking?

A piglet, one of the ungreased ones, scurried across the row, appearing and disappearing like magic. Ayden reached out his *earth-sense* to the piglet—*calm, fatigue, hunger*—urges that might send the baby home to its mother, but the tiny brain was not like the wolves or horses. Its train of thought, if any, scattered like grain across the ground for hens to peck.

Senses alive, he tracked the small animal through the tall, dry stalks and across the narrow aisles. He trampled the dead vegetation, burning out his anger at the silly girls who'd caused this disaster.

The sudden awareness of others nearby halted his headlong rush.

Two humans—*men*—waited with their animals on the far side of the field near the road that bordered Brown's farm.

Closer at hand, two more people—*one a woman*—moved toward each other through the dry cornstalks.

I should only sense piglets in this part of the field. Could this be a lover's meeting?

That seemed unlikely, even to an almost fifteen-year-old boy. Even in his wildest imaginings, he could not conjure a romantic encounter in a cornfield.

His side vision registered a movement, and he turned his head.

A large black sow ambled across the row then faded into the stalks beyond, followed by a woman in a flowing white gown. Chills raced down his arms as the apparition disappeared into the field toward the couple ahead.

Piglets forgotten, Ayden eased his way between the rows, following the lady in white toward the couple's meeting point.

***

Margaret James

—

The sky darkened. The heavy, threatening clouds that had lined the western horizon on their way to the farm rolled across it, bringing with them the scent of rain. Dry corn rows rustled in the brisk breeze and made it impossible to hear piglets running in the field.

Or Ayden. I'd best turn back or chance a soaking.

Ahead of her, two figures crossed her path. The first, a black sow, followed immediately by a pale woman in a flowing white gown. The woman paused, her gaze directed beyond Margaret, and slowly raised her hand to point down the row.

Margaret spun on her heel, chilled to the bone by the apparition, and bounced off the chest of a strange man. She struck him with such force she stumbled back, fell to the ground, and rubbed her nose.

The stranger laughed. His gaping mouth displayed missing and rotted teeth. The breeze lifted white hair and tossed it about his head like a crazed ghoul. "Look what I found."

Not a ghoul.

Margaret scrambled backward, rolled to rise to her feet, but was knocked back down by a boot to her backside.

"And they said there weren't no women here."

She twisted to watch him and kicked his hand when he reached for the hem of her skirt. "Don't touch me."

"Mighty prissy." He leaned forward and grabbed her boot when she kicked. "That ain't nice. You must like it rough. I know I sure do."

His chuckle turned into a surprised grunt as he was knocked back by a man who burst from the adjacent row.

"Ayden?" Margaret scrambled to her feet, eyeing the two men who wrestled on the ground.

"Go," Ayden yelled at her. "Run." The ghoulish man's fist knocked Ayden's head back.

She ran past where they fought, then stopped in the row to watch.

There must be something I can do.

Ayden fell back across the row.

Her assailant thrashed to his feet and picked up the long rifle Ayden had knocked from his hands. "This won't be pretty, but I'm sure gonna like it." He lifted the rifle butt to his shoulder and squinted down the barrel at Ayden.

Ayden gained his feet and lifted his hand toward the rifle barrel. "Don't shoot," he warned.

With a grin, the white-haired man squeezed the trigger. As the firing pin struck the cap, the gunpowder exploded backward, blasting the breech plug into the attacker's face. Smoke and fire followed the dead man to the ground.

Ayden closed his fingers into a fist, and the fire ceased. His gaze turned from the man on the ground to Margaret, and his eyes widened with astonished recognition.

"Run back to the farm." He closed the distance between them. "There are two more of these men in the field."

"What? How do you know?"

"They came to the farm after the moon gathering." He gripped her upper arm and pushed her ahead of him. "Run, Margaret."

She lifted her skirt and dashed through the corn. Freezing rain, driven by the wind, pelted her head. The row curved, limiting her vision, her heart thundered in her ears, then she was out of the corn. She stumbled to a stop and gazed around the empty yard.

The members at the Samhain celebration had retreated inside to escape the storm. No one would have heard her cry for help.

"Let's get inside." Ayden took her hand and led her toward the house. "Leader Brown needs to be told what's happened."

***

Chantal James

—

"This is a list of the properties Sully owns." Chantal paused and looked Garrett in the eye. "I meant to say *owned*. The listings marked with an 'x' I wish to sell immediately. The rest I will retain—for now."

"You're speaking as a proxy for your sons?" Garrett looked up from the paperwork Chantal had placed before him and peered at her over his wire-rimmed glasses. "Widows don't own—"

"I know. I know. And yes, as a proxy." She brushed her skirt in irritation. "You will function as our attorney and manage the sale of those properties, to include collecting the proceeds and depositing the funds as directed."

"You mean, function as your sons' attorney?"

Chantal took a short sharp breath through her nose and bared her teeth as she forced a bitter smile at Garrett Brown. "I believe you know what I meant." Her tone held a warning.

Garrett grinned at her, unperturbed. "I do indeed. However, I also know the law." He moved the list and the stack of deeds in front of her. "Your signature will not be enough. You'll need both of your sons' signatures on each deed of sale. If the property is still in Sully's name, you need a transfer of ownership to your sons and a certificate of death."

"Fine. Obtain everything you need. Then have the boys execute deeds of sale for all the properties, including this farm. You retain the paperwork until I advise you to sell each property. Once a property sells, you fill in the price, buyer, and date. It's as easy as that."

"You're asking me to circumvent the law, Chantal."

"If my sons asked you to do this, would you still be evading the law?

Garrett shook his head. "No, but I'm not sure there's a point to this." He tossed his reading glasses onto the desk, steepled his fingers, and gazed at Chantal over his hands. "I will get the titles changed to show Bern and Bay as the owners. I will draw up sale documents for the properties *they wish to sell now*. I will discuss the process of selling real estate with your sons, and I will go to each parcel, boarding house, or restaurant to post the property for sale. When a buyer comes forward, Bay and Bern will execute the deed of sale and collect the proceeds."

"I don't understand why you won't do as I ask."

"And I don't understand why you want to make this more difficult than it already is." He rose from his chair and paced behind the desk. "Is it that you don't trust your sons?"

"Of course, I trust them. My boys will always do as I ask."

Garrett paused and raised one brow at Chantal.

Before either could respond, the door to the office burst opened, and Ayden and Margaret swept in.

Chantal came to her feet and blinked with shock at her daughter's appearance. "Your dress!"

Garrett rounded the desk. "What's happened?"

Ayden picked up a colorful knit blanket from the sofa beside the door and wrapped it around Margaret's wet shoulders. "The slave catchers are back. One of them, the middle brother, I think, trapped Margaret in the cornfield."

"What were you doing in the cornfield?" Chantal demanded of her daughter.

"I thought to help catch piglets." Margaret's teeth chattered. She moved to the fire burning low in the office hearth.

"Piglets?" Chantal muttered and looked to Garrett and Ayden for an explanation.

"Where are the men now?" Garrett plucked the long rifle from the mantel and checked the load.

"The brother who attacked Margaret is dead in the field."

Garrett looked up from the long gun and narrowed his eyes at Ayden.

Chantal's gaze shot from the young man beside the door to her daughter. "Dead how?"

"His rifle blew up in his face," Margaret replied over her shoulder.

"Were the other brothers there? Did they see this happen?" Garrett asked.

"No." Ayden shook his head. "They were at the edge of the field along the farm road when the breech blew, but they had to have heard the blast."

"But you were there?" Garrett paused at the door beside Ayden.

"Yes. I stopped the man from hurting Margaret. He fired his rifle at me because of that."

Pounding rattled the porch door.

Garrett stared at Ayden for a moment, then looked at the women. "The older brother will ask questions. It would be best if Margaret speaks to him and doesn't mention Ayden."

"Why not?" Chantal demanded.

"The slavers have seen Ayden. Besides, Ayden and the catcher are both angry. Unfounded accusations will make matters worse. We want this man to take his brother and leave without question." He held out his arm to Margaret. "Your daughter is shaken. Her account will be convincing." He opened the office door to curious faces. "All is well, folks. Margaret witnessed a tragic accident in the cornfield." He waved Margaret forward. "But she is fine." He looked back at Ayden. "Clean yourself up. Stay out of sight."

Garrett crossed the kitchen, staging Margaret in her mother's arms behind him. He rested the rifle beside the table then opened the door. "Mr. Finley. I thought we might see you tonight," Garrett said, his tone grave.

"I found Clifford in your field with tracks coming this way." Fierce anger and grief etched the slave catcher's face. "I want to know what happened."

"We just heard about this ourselves." Garrett nodded and held out his arm. "Margaret, will you tell Mr. Finley what you told us?"

***

Margaret James

—

Margaret nodded, stepped out of Chantal's protective embrace and into Garrett's. "Yes." She faced the man standing in the doorway. Her body refused to stop trembling.

An older image of the ghoul in the cornfield stared at her. His long rain-plastered white hair clung to his face and neck. He held his long gun with two hands as he glared into her eyes. "Well, speak up."

"I r-ran into your brother while chasing a p-piglet in the cornfield. I f-fell down." Her face heated, and she looked at the floor. "He laughed and made a r-rude comment." She looked up at the man in the doorway. "He reached for my skirt, then s-something startled him."

"What startled him?"

"One of the piglets, perhaps." Margaret lifted one shoulder. "I don't know. He raised the r-rifle, and it exploded in his f-face." She covered her mouth with her hand. The trembling increased as tears slid down her face. "I didn't know what to do—so I ran back here. I know I should have tried to help him."

Garrett turned Margaret toward her mother.

Chantal wrapped her distraught daughter in her arms.

"Do you need help getting him out of the field?" Garrett indicated the small group of people who had taken shelter from the weather in his house. "I have guests who can help."

"No." Clem Finley shook his head. "I jus' needed to know how Cliff ended. Now I do." He rubbed his nose with a gloved hand and blinked. "Clyde and I will take Clifford home. We won't bother you again." He touched the brim of his rain-soaked hat, turned, and disappeared into the freezing rain.

Chapter 8

Ayden MacKenna

—

Ayden had known it would rain sometime that afternoon. They all had. The weight of moisture in the air made its presence known, especially to those with *water-skill*. The drop in temperature, however, surprised everyone.

The piglets found their way back to Fat Sal, and the apples were scooped from the barrel at the first sign of rain. Food brought to the Samhain celebration by coven members filled the kitchen counters, and a makeshift corridor of rain gear over ropes allowed passage from the house to the large barn. Although it should have been a muddy mess, *earth-* and *water-skilled* members kept the passageway dry, while *fire-* and *air-skilled* kept it warm.

Had the weather held fair, the midday meal would have been taken at the tables outside, and a large Samhain bonfire built in the yard before sunset. As it was, a lesser fire burned in the center of the pentacle and drew both diners and revelers to the barn.

Seated along the back wall on a bale of hay, Ayden scooped corn chowder with a piece of roll and listened to the musicians. Musical members played the concertina, two guitars, and a fiddle, creating spirited music in the corner. Younger children and three couples danced to the tunes.

Farm families who lived nearby packed their wagons, wished everyone a happy Samhain, and headed home when the rain first began. Those who remained hailed from Boston or further away would spend the evening at the farm to head home in the light of day.

Ayden's parents danced to the music, unaware of anything but each other.

As though she sensed the touch of his gaze, his mother waved her fingers at him and smiled.

Ayden grinned at her and gave her a nod.

Across the barn, Margaret, her mother, and Leader Brown entered the building. Brown spoke briefly to Chantal, then headed toward the fire in the center of the room.

Chantal surveyed the gathering, then proceeded to where her sons ate, on the other side of the musicians.

Margaret waved to several people but didn't pause to chat. Her destination never wavered, nor did her gaze. She headed straight for him.

Ayden set his bowl aside and waited.

"Hello," she said and blushed. "I never had the chance to thank you. You saved me."

"I—uh," Ayden stammered, his face heating. "And you told a lie to save me."

"Not a complete lie. I merely left you out of the story. Everything else happened just as I said."

"Have you eaten?"

"Yes. In the house."

In the corner, across from the musicians, a group gathered around one of the elders. The old witch made a production of seating himself, then grinned at the youngsters who settled around him.

"Let's listen to his ghost stories," Margaret urged.

Ayden nodded, and they found seats at the back of the group around the storyteller.

"As ye know, at this time of year, the veil between the world of the living and the dead is very thin." Dressed in his coven robe and long white beard, the elder rolled his eyes and shook his head at the children. "It's a time to be wary and mind your mums, for they already know, don't they?"

The children nodded and looked at each other for confirmation.

Margaret took Ayden's arm.

"The *Púcai now, they* steal those poor unwary children away from their homes without a fuss. They are shapeshifters and will trick you by changing themselves into a dog, or a horse, or even someone you know." He wiggled his eyebrows at the younger children.

"But the most frightening spirit of all is the dreaded White Lady. She's sometimes called The Lady Gwyn. She wanders the country at this time of year, searching for travelers or those up to no good. Her tailless black sow always accompanies the White Lady." He raised one brow and leaned forward to whisper, "Never let her catch you."

Margaret tugged on his sleeve, leaned close, and whispered in his ear, "I saw her."

A shiver ran the length of Ayden's frame. He came to his feet, taking Margaret's hands and raising her to her feet as well. "I did too. In the cornfield."

"Yes." Margaret nodded as they moved away from the ghost stories. "I saw the black sow first and thought it might be the mother of the piglets, but then the white lady drifted into the row in front of me." She pulled him to a stop. "It wasn't just the rain that made me spin so fast and run into that, that—man."

"Shh, now. It's behind us." Ayden returned to the haybale and pulled her down to sit beside him. Hands folded together, he leaned forward and touched his forehead to hers. "I was angry in the field. Angry at those girls and at missing the festivities. I tried to reach out with my mind to find the piglets, but instead, I sensed people in the field."

He lowered his voice to reach only her ear. "When I opened my eyes, something gossamer white blurred past—The White Lady, I imagine. She flowed through the cornstalks. I followed her and found you." He stared into Margaret's wide dark eyes filled with unshed tears. "You're well, Margaret. So am I. Don't think about it anymore."

Margaret nodded and brushed the heel of her hand beneath her downcast eyes. "You're right."

"There you are." Leader Brown halted beside the young couple. "I'm rounding up the inductees. I want to conduct the initiations while many of the members remain at hand." He motioned to the open door. "The rain has stopped, and quite a few folks have said they intend to chance the ride home before they lose the light of day."

Ayden reached for his robe folded neatly on the haybale.

"You won't need that," Brown said over his shoulder as he moved on to another inductee. "This will be more celebration and less ceremony."

Margaret stood and brushed the hay from her skirt. "Good luck, and congratulations."

"Thank you. Do you think your family will stay at the farm tonight?"

"I think so." Margaret glanced over her shoulder toward her brothers and mother. "It's a bad night to travel for several reasons." She gave him a half-smile, then hurried across the room to her family.

"Can I have your attention, please?" Garrett stood in front of the pentacle fire—hands raised. "I'm sorry to interrupt your merriment, but we have an order of business to address before the evening continues. I know some of you intend to leave for home shortly, and at least half have already wished us well and taken their leave during this break in the storm." He looked around the large room as though taking stock of the revelers. "Of our eleven young initiates, we have four here, and they will be received into our coven this afternoon. In addition, we are fortunate to have two adults who wish to become a part of our family as well."

The music wound down to an end while he spoke. The children around the storyteller jumped to their feet and wove through the small crowd seeking their parents—a loose circle of members formed around the edge of the pentacle.

"This will be an informal ceremony, and everyone may attend, even the children. Are my lieutenants present? Good. Please call your directions and seal our circle."

Four members stepped forward wearing their long robes and cowls and moved to each of the cardinal points on the pentagram.

The woman who faced east raised her arms and recited her invocation.

※

"Spirits of the East, we call you.

"Attend us, Elements of Air.

"Surround us with your protection,

"The breath of life and transformation.

"Share with us sacred Samhain, the end of harvest,

"And grant us your blessings for the New Year."

✳

A whisper of air whirled around the barn. It carried the scent of pine, and freshness filled the space.

A child squealed with surprise and delight.

The man facing south raised his arms and called out.

✳

"Spirits of the South, we call you.

"Attend us, Elements of Fire.

"Surround us with your protection and offer us

"The light that banishes darkness during the blackest of nights.

"Share with us sacred Samhain, the end of harvest,

"And grant us your blessings for the New Year."

✳

The fire at the center of the pentacle flared, rising to the rafters before dying down. A whiff of home fires joined the pine-scented air circling the barn.

The next man stepped forward.

✳

"Spirits of the West, we call you.

"Attend us, Elements of Water.

"Surround us with your protection and offer us

"The cleansing rain that replenishes the earth.

"Share with us sacred Samhain, the end of harvest,

"And grant us your blessings for the New Year."

✳

From the smoke hole in the roof came a spray of moisture. It joined the breeze of pine scent, fragrant smoke, and the promise of spring.

The final lieutenant raised her hands.

✳

"Spirits of the North, we call you.

"Attend us, Elements of Earth.

"Surround us with your protection and offer us

"The strength of stone to compel our purpose.

"Share with us sacred Samhain, the end of harvest,

"And grant us your blessings for the New Year."

✳

Dust on the ground lifted in a ripple and spread from the north point across the star pattern. The swirling air picked up the scent of earth and folded it into its fragrant potpourri before it stilled.

Leader Brown nodded to each lieutenant and looked with pride at the people gathered around the sacred circle. Instead of raising his arms, he bowed his head.

✳

"God and Goddess, be welcome in our hearts,

"Lord and Lady, in all aspects of your creation,

"Hold us in your protection, and offer us

"The reborn spirit of our father,

"And the loving embrace of our mother,

"Share with us sacred Samhain, the end of harvest,

"And grant us your blessings for the New Year."

✳

A cheer went up from the observers, both coven members and guests. Children jumped up and down with excitement to witness one of the magical mysteries of the coven.

"Let's bring this circle to order and conduct our business so we may get back to celebrating this sacred holiday."

The lieutenants remained in their corners facing the central fire, arms tucked in their sleeves, heads bowed. They appeared the guardians of their cardinal points.

Garrett did not wear a robe. His white shirtsleeves rolled to just beneath his elbows, with suspenders securing his chestnut brown trousers. "Initiation into our coven is a solemn undertaking, but it is also a cause for celebration.

As I said before, we had eleven initiates, but only four remain here today and two adults who seek membership in our ranks.

"We shall welcome the adults first.

"Warren Johnson is a carpenter like his father. He and his wife, Roberta, come to us from the State of New York. They are sponsored into our coven by Wrigley Johnson, Warren's brother.

"Warren and Roberta, please step forward."

The young couple held hands as they stepped into the circle and approached Leader Brown.

"I hope you're enjoying yourself today," Leader Brown greeted the initiates. "Even with the rain, we are having a very merry celebration."

"We're having a grand time today," Warren admitted with a shy smile at his wife.

Ayden watched with curiosity. He'd noticed them during the festival and would have never guessed they were married because of their young age, perhaps fifteen or sixteen years. "Warren's primary skill is *Air*. Roberta's is *Fire*," Leader Brown continued. "Please welcome Warren and Roberta into our coven family."

Leader Brown shook their hands as the coven applauded. When the young couple had left the pentacle, and the crowd grew silent, Garrett grinned. "Now to our young apprentices."

"Gordon Carmichael, Milton Kohler, Suzanne Cumberland, and Ayden MacKenna. Please enter our circle." He waited until the four initiates were in a line facing him. "Would the sponsors for these young people please come forward?"

Leader Brown nodded as the last parent stepped into the pentacle. "Learning to be a member of this coven, or any coven, is not a journey a young man or woman must make alone.

"As sponsors, it is your responsibility to teach our newest members as much as you can about their skills. Even if their primary and yours are different, you will have more fully explored the entire spectrum of elemental skills as adults. Your lesser skills will be just as valuable for training these young people as your primaries. Teach them restraint. Teach them respect.

And most of all, teach them to never use their enormous advantage against the unskilled.

"Never speak of this coven to those who are unable to understand our need for like-minded companions and the bond that those of us who wield magic enjoy."

"And now, let us welcome into our fold, Gordon, whose primary skill is *Fire*. Milton, whose primary skill is *Earth*. Suzanne, whose primary skill is *Water*, and Ayden, whose primary skill is *Fire*." Leader Brown lifted his arms, and his voice filled the large enclosure, "Please welcome all of tonight's initiates into our coven family."

The cheers from two-dozen people shook the rafters. Fist-sized fireballs exploded into sparkling colors overhead and floated to the ground as colorful cool ash. Streamers of water circled above their heads, changing shapes, and reflecting the colors of the ash. Vibrations drummed beneath their feet.

Ayden's heart filled with a feeling of fellowship equal only to the sense of belonging he felt with his family. He met their proud gazes and knew his smile matched theirs. He turned, taking in the joyous salute, and found Margaret.

Clapping gloved hands, she stood between her brothers and her mother. She had grown so much since he last saw her. She was maturing toward the woman he sometimes glimpsed in the fire. That they belonged together, he had no doubt. Someday, the girl bouncing on her toes, cheering his name would be his wife.

They grinned at each other.

The affection Margaret felt for him shone from her eyes.

Just then, her mother wrapped her arm around Margaret's shoulder, turning her toward the door.

Bernard grabbed his brother's arm, interrupting his fire display, and pulled him along behind their mother.

Chantal stood aside as her children left the barn. In the doorway, she turned her critical gaze on Ayden. For several seconds, the two matched stares, then surprisingly, Chantal dropped her glare and departed the building.

Chapter 9

Ayden MacKenna

—

May 1845 – Near Boston Harbor

Ayden heaved the heavy burlap sack filled with barley over his shoulder and carried it out the back of the store to the buyer's wagon. He placed this bag alongside the others. "One more."

The brewer nodded and snapped his pocket watch closed. "Double time, lad. I've got to be home for supper, or the missus won't be happy."

After Ayden loaded the last bag, the patron flipped him a half dime. "Tell Murphy I'll see him next month."

"I will, and thank you, sir." Ayden pushed the coin into his pocket and returned to the stockroom. Without pause, he took up the broom and swept the dry chaff from the grain out the door, then secured the back exit. He passed through the curtain to the front of the store while he took off his work apron, then hung it on a hook beside the curtain.

Behind the counter, Mr. Murphy called goodbye to a customer as he sorted the woman's payment. He looked up and smiled at Ayden, then back down at the coins. He made a mark in his ledger, then returned his attention to his store clerk. "Tillerman get his barley?"

"He did. He said he'd see you next month."

"I'm sure he will." Murphy closed the drawer then smiled at Ayden. "Give the store a final sweep. Then you can go."

"It's still early." Ayden picked up the broom, gathered the dust on the floor with long strokes, and occasionally glanced over at Murphy.

"What is it, boy?"

"Nothing really, sir. I only want to remind you that I will be out of town with my folks for a few days. I'll be back to work on Tuesday morning."

"I remember, lad, now get on with you and enjoy the nice weather."

"Thank you, sir," Ayden called as he slipped on his jacket and hurried from the shop.

Outside, the clang of metal on metal tolled down the street as the blacksmith beat his heavy hammer against red-hot steel on the anvil. The front of the smith's shop, generally closed to the walkway, stood open to catch the pleasant spring breeze. The corner boasted the blacksmith shop, a wheelwright, and the farrier where Ayden's father had found employment four years ago.

But it was the furnace behind the muscular workman that seized Ayden's attention. He stumbled to a stop as the flame captured his gaze. He rarely sought visions anymore. His failure to prevent the death of Margaret's father haunted him.

Margaret no longer attended coven meetings, only her brothers and occasionally her mother, but never her.

The thought of Margaret quickened his pulse, and the shadows moving in the flames of the forge resolved into her face, but this wasn't the Margaret he remembered.

Her hair, always combed and braided, hung in loose waves around her face. Her dark eyes sparkled, and her swollen lips held a mischievous smile. When she leaned forward, Ayden realized she wore no bodice, and the unbuttoned shirt, *his shirt*, gapped open, revealing the curve of her breast and more. Although the visions had no sound, he could read her lips, *"Don't worry so much. Everything will be all right. I love you, Ayden."*

"Hey boy, are you ill?"

Startled, Ayden blinked at the blacksmith. Instead of gawking from the street, he stood in the man's shop, past the short counter, halfway to the forge. He took a step back and rubbed his forehead. "I'm sorry."

"Is there something you need?" The man picked up the metal from the anvil with large tongs and pushed it into the forge fire, then returned his attention to Ayden.

"No." Ayden backed from the shop. "Sorry," he called to the smith again.

He'd never had a vision like this. Not that he hadn't thought about kissing and touching a girl, especially Margaret. At seventeen, those fantasies were familiar, even though he hadn't set eyes on Margaret in almost three years. Still, he'd never imagined anything like what he witnessed just now.

He turned down the next street and worked his way south and west from the North End where his family lived, toward the wealthier homes on Beacon Hill—and Margaret. The coven meet was two weeks away, but he knew she would not attend with her brothers.

I must see her now.

His fast pace turned into a trot as he dodged businessmen who strolled downtown with their walking sticks and top hats.

When he reached the Common, he slowed, replaying Margaret's description of where she lived as best he could. He knew the street name but was uncertain of the house number. Three blocks from the park, he turned left and studied the home entrances. Although all the homes shared a similar facade, Margaret spoke of her mother's red flowering plant, which set on the front stoop once the weather warmed.

Halfway down the long block, he spotted crimson blossoms beside a blue door.

His gaze darted to the upstairs windows, and although the curtains were open, nothing moved.

He continued up the walk but realized he couldn't knock on the door. Margaret's mother would demand to know what he wanted, and what could he say? Besides, coming straight from work, he wasn't dressed to call on anyone, much less Miss Margaret James of Beacon Hill.

As he turned away, the front door opened. He vaulted the iron rail between the houses and pressed tight to the tall decorative shrub beside the black fence.

A housemaid, basket over her arm and a white scarf on her head, stepped out to the porch then paused. She glanced over her shoulder, nodded, and hurried down the walk and up the street.

A moment later, Margaret appeared on the porch with a small watering can.

Intent on catching her attention, and no other should her mother or brothers be nearby, Ayden captured the first droplets of water as they spilled from the spout and spun them in a wide spiral before they fell to the plant.

Margaret ceased watering the plant, and her gaze lifted to the upper floors, then scanned the street. She hesitated a moment, then closed her eyes. When they opened wide with surprise, her head turned, and she smiled at Ayden with a mischievous grin. "You can still surprise me."

"Shh." Ayden held a finger over his lips. "Is there a place we may speak in private?"

Even as she narrowed her eyes, her smile widened, and she gave him a slow nod. "Meet me in the alleyway behind my house." Her skirt whirled, and the door shut behind her.

Adrenaline quickened Ayden's pace while worry clouded his mind.

The narrow alley behind her house would be too exposed.

The conversation he intended to have with Margaret required privacy. He was already uncertain how he could relay his recent vision or his feelings for her. He most certainly did not want any interruptions.

He rounded the corner and trotted down the alley.

I should have counted the houses.

He slowed and brushed damp hair from his eyes. The pace he kept on his trot across downtown, and now the run around the long Beacon Hill block, made the refreshing spring afternoon feel like a hot and humid summer day. He opened his coat then slipped it from his shoulders.

Although his mother had mended his father's old single-breasted frock coat for him, she'd needed to widen the shoulders. She used pieces from the coat's skirt leftover from shortening the older garment to a more modern style, then lengthened the arms by adding an exaggerated cuff at the wrist.

Ayden waited in the alleyway, his coat folded over his arm. The tall houses on both sides of the cobbled way blocked the breeze.

A gate rattled behind him, and he turned on his heel.

Margaret eased the latch down then hurried past him. She opened the neighbor's gate and motioned for him to follow. "This is the Prescott home. They own ships. My friend is away for several months, on an extended tour of Europe."

She pulled a ring of keys from her pocket and opened a door on the side of the carriage house. "Years ago, Mr. Prescott added a room for their coachman, but Mrs. Prescott prefers to use the livery by the church." The door swung open, and Margaret slipped inside.

A flame flared from the wooden match between her fingers. With a wave of her hand, three small oil lamps glowed with light. "My friend gave me a second set of keys." She jingled the keys in her hand. "We used to play dolls here."

"You manipulate *Fire* easily." Ayden stepped inside the room. Three dolls stared back at him from the mattress on the floor.

The small lodging shared a wall with what had once been the stable. The tiny single-room apartment boasted a small stove, the doll mattress, and a table with two chairs.

"*Fire-skill* runs in the family." She smiled up at him. "I can manipulate all the elements a bit. Mother says my secondary skill will become apparent soon, I hope."

"Congratulations."

"Thank you."

The late afternoon light shone through the dirty window, highlighting specks of dust that floated between them.

Margaret's eyes were wide and dark, the pupil large in the dusky light when she looked up at him. "Was there something you wanted to tell me?" She moved closer.

Ayden nodded. "Yes. I—" He swallowed. His mouth suddenly dry. He folded his jacket and set it on the table. "I think it's important that you know, my visions are often of you." His face warmed, and he was glad for the shadows.

"I believe in my heart that you and I shall marry one day." He lifted his gaze to hers. "And my feelings for you, at times, overcome my good sense, like coming here."

"Ayden—"

"If we're caught, alone in this manner, your reputation—"

She crossed the small room and laid her delicate finger across his lips to silence his concerns. "No one will discover us, I assure you." She took a small step back and folded her hands together. "You mean more to me than you know. I realize there has never been a time we might speak in private or confess our feelings, but I swear to you now, just the sight of you after so long gladdens my heart. I shall live for the time I may see you again." She worked one of the keys free from the ring. "Here is the second key. We may meet here and speak in private whenever we wish."

"But Margaret—"

"Look, we can leave each other messages." Margaret pulled a small stack of paper from the nightstand drawer, waved them then put them back. "There are pencils in there as well." She turned to the bed. "We can hide our missives here." She picked up one of the dolls and pulled off its head, showing him the hollow inside. "Roll up your note and tuck it inside." She restored the doll and placed it on the bed. "Even if someone should come in, our message would be secure."

Ayden nodded and slipped the key into his pocket. "You are the only girl for me, Margaret. I know you are." He took her hand. "I would very much like to kiss you."

"You want to kiss me?" Her excited movements and chatter stilled, and her eyes grew wide. "Now?"

"Very much so." He took her hand and drew her close. "But only with your permission."

Margaret nodded, tipped her head back, and closed her eyes.

Ayden lowered his head and pressed his lips to hers, but it was not the passionate kiss he'd witnessed in the fire. He raised his head and looked into her open eyes. "I should go."

Margaret nodded with disappointment. "When might I see you again?"

Ayden lifted her hand and kissed the back of her fingers. "I'll try to leave work early again tomorrow, but that is not a sure thing. We should set a time to meet again right now."

"Yes, we should." Her brow furrowed in confusion. "You're employed?"

Ayden smiled. "You sound surprised."

"It's just that—my brothers aren't employed, not like that, and they're older than you."

"Your brothers are Boston Brahmin. I have to work to make money." His smile faded. "One of the many reasons your mother will never approve of a match between us. Now kiss me quickly, for I must leave."

"But—"

His lips caught hers partially open, and the sweetness of her mouth surprised him. His inhalation drew their lips tighter together. He groaned as his arms tightened around her and the kiss deepened until Margaret pushed against his shoulders. He lifted his head and looked down at her flushed face. "Oh Margaret, I'm so sorry."

"No. Don't be sorry. I couldn't breathe, and I can't return home in disarray."

"I think you're supposed to breathe." He released her and stepped back. Her face was flushed, but her hair and clothing did not need repair. "You look fine."

She nodded and felt her hair, then brushed at her skirt. "You leave first. I'll lock up after you're gone. You have the key?"

He touched his trouser pocket then picked up his jacket from the table. "I do." Their gazes held. "One week from tonight at midnight, we'll meet back here. I'm not sure I could wait longer than that."

Margaret nodded. "One week." She stepped forward and reached up to kiss the side of his face. "Don't be late."

Ayden fought the urge to take her in his arms again, but daylight awaited him outside of the door. Darkness would lessen the risk they took. Giddy with the knowledge she returned his affection, he slipped from the carriage apartment.

Ayden hurried to the gate and into the alley. He debated with himself if he should wait and speak to her again in the narrow passageway but realized it would be foolish. In the end, he hurried to the corner and angled across Beacon Hill toward his home on the north side.

***

Margaret James

—

Margaret stared at the closed door, her fingers lightly touching her swollen lips.

He loves me.

Her knees and stomach trembled, and she closed her eyes for a moment to relive his embrace.

One day they would wed.

Margaret's heart soared as she opened her eyes and looked around the room. She'd bring fresh bedding and a few jars of water. She turned to survey her childhood playrooms and her gaze caught on the bed. It was a child's mat now, but she could fix that too.

Satisfied with her plans, she snuffed the lantern flames with a thought and left the small apartment. While she locked the door, Margaret reminded herself to bring several old newspapers to block any light that might shine from the windows at midnight. Without further hesitation, she hurried out the gate and back to her house.

***

Ayden MacKenna

—

At home, Ayden hung his jacket on a peg by the door. The warm scent of pork and beans and fresh-baked bread filled the air.

In the kitchen, his mother and father spoke softly.

Ayden hesitated to break their concentration on each other.

His father knelt and pressed his lips to his mother's stomach as his mother beamed a smile at his bent head.

She's pregnant. The vision was true, and I'll have a little brother.

Rachael lifted her gaze from his father and saw him. "Ayden." She held out her hand. "Come. I have news."

Large families within the skilled community were nonexistent. The James household, with three offspring, was the largest he'd ever seen. Typically, the God and Goddess bestowed only one child to magically endowed parents, if any. That his mother would have another child was indeed a blessing.

Ayden took her hand as Lyam came to his feet, and they all shared a hug.

"My vision proved correct then." Ayden smiled at the joy on his mother's face.

"You had a vision?" she asked.

"On our way to Boston, before we stopped at the Brown farm. You don't remember?"

Lyam chuckled. "That was years ago, but yes, I remember now."

"It will be a boy, born in the winter," Ayden added.

"By my count, near the end of November." Rachael turned to the stove. "Take a seat. Dinner is ready."

"I have news as well." Ayden sat beside his father as his mother dished up dinner into bowls. "I intend to court and marry Margaret James." He picked up his spoon, but the silence in the room forced his gaze to lift with caution.

Both parents stared at him with dismay.

"That will be a difficult match for you." His mother finally offered as she took her seat. "I imagine her mother will expect young Margaret to marry a Brahmin with wealth and position."

"Chantal will forbid this marriage out of hand," his father stated as he placed a square section of cornbread on his plate. "We all know how she feels about our family."

Anger flared in Ayden's chest, and he clenched his jaw. "So, you're against us too?"

"Not at all," Rachael soothed. "We just want you to understand the difficulties you'll face. Her family will be firmly against this match."

"And my family?" Ayden looked from his mother to his father.

"We only want what is best for you," Lyam said.

"And above all else," his mother continued, "we want you to be happy."

A week later, Ayden watched the candle flame on his nightstand while he lay in bed. He tried again to discover how he and Margaret's relationship would progress, but the images never appeared in any reasonable order. Sometimes they shared a meal and talked, holding hands. At other times they kissed.

He concentrated on the flame as tonight's vision emerged.

Inside their secret hideaway, Margaret unbuttoned her jacket and untucked the short camisole from the waistband on her skirt. Their lips met with deep passion as he pulled the pins from her hair. Together they lowered themselves to the bed. Their lips clung together, and the kiss deepened—mouths open, they stole the breath from each other as the excitement of the moment overwhelmed them both.

His hand slipped beneath her camisole, pushing up the material until he exposed her breast. Tenderly, he lowered his head to her nipple and circled it with his tongue.

She arched her back and gasped with pleasure, encouraging his advance.

He took the hardened nub between his fingers as his lips found hers once more.

Beneath the sheet, his physical reaction to the vision startled him, and he groaned. His hand slid down his bare stomach to his erection just as a knock sounded at the door. He closed his eyes to feign sleep as his bedroom door eased open.

"Are you still awake?" his mother whispered.

Ayden blinked his eyes and raised his head. "Did you need me?"

"No, no. I just saw the light and thought you might have fallen asleep with the candle burning, and you had." She pinched out the flame from the doorway. "Good night, sweetheart."

Once the door closed, Ayden rolled to his back and angled his arm across his eyes. All evidence of his arousal fled the moment his mother spoke.

The vision was not about tonight. I can't go to Margaret with unrealistic expectations.

He knew he couldn't display his vision-inspired lust to Margaret. His beloved was young and innocent. Their physical relationship must progress naturally, much like the love they shared had grown over time. And even though he did not wish to consummate their passion before they wed, the vision in flame appeared to indicate otherwise.

Ayden lay in bed for an hour after his parents had doused their light and gone to bed. When the house echoed with his father's familiar snore, he rose and dressed in the dark. With the stealth worthy of a criminal act, he opened his bedroom window, slipped through, and silently lowered himself to the ground. He eased the window closed with enormous care, leaving a fingerwidth's span to reopen upon his return.

The waxing gibbous moon kept him company as he hurried up the hill through the late-night streets. Sounds from the boisterous waterside taverns faded behind him as the neighborhood changed to modest businesses and then to finer homes.

As Ayden turned down the alley that led to their rendezvous location, a dog's deep bark broke the night's silence. Startled, he stopped and crouched into the shadows beside a stone wall.

An angry command yelled through an open window quieted the animal who paced beyond a nearby fence, sniffing the night air. The beast huffed and growled at the unfamiliar scent in the alleyway.

Ayden swallowed. Any movement might set the beast off again and bring his owner. To be discovered creeping along a quiet Beacon Hill alley in the middle of the night would mean arrest as a prowler and possible thief. He could never share the real reason he crept in the dark.

A door beyond the fence opened, and the dog huffed again at the alley.

"Get in here, Sampson, you dumb animal. Leave those raccoons alone. You're a danged nuisance...." The man scolded the dog until the slammed door cut off his voice.

With a new appreciation for what they risked, Ayden continued down the alley to Margaret's neighbors. He eased through the gate, into the backyard, and rounded the carriage house. The eaves shadowed the door from the moon, bathing him in darkness. He felt for the handle, and the door opened slightly. A soft light escaped through the crack. Without hesitation, he slipped inside the small apartment and closed the door.

Chapter 10

Margaret James

—

May 1845 – Beacon Hill

Margaret straightened the cuffs on her blouse again and brushed at her skirt. She surveyed the small apartment to assure herself nothing more need be done before Ayden arrived. She had come early to arrange the cut flowers and set the two oil lamps low. They filled the small place with a soft glow and a sweet fragrance.

Knowing she would need to rise from bed and dress without light, she had folded away a simple outfit in advance—an old skirt she could wear without a corset and a blouse that buttoned up the front. Beneath those, her simple cotton nightgown functioned as both camisole and slip. Lastly, she wore a pair of old house slippers instead of her boots.

Slipping out of the house had been simple. Her brothers, away on business for her mother, would not be awake to discover her sneaking down the kitchen stairs. Her yard, the alley, and the carriage house playroom were as familiar to her as her bedroom.

Impatient now for Ayden to arrive, she pulled her long, loose hair to one side and twisted it into a thick coil.

I hate to wait. It gives me too much time to think.

Anxious tremors assailed her stomach, and she released the thick curl and clutched her hands together in her lap.

Outside, the soft snick of the gate latch dropping brought her to her feet.

What if someone saw me leave the house?

What if someone followed me? How will I explain?

Her breath caught in her throat as the door eased open.

Ayden's conspiratorial grin brought a soft sob of relief. She dabbed tears from the corner of her eyes while he removed his coat. "I'm glad it's you."

"Who else?" Ayden hung his jacket on the back of the chair. He stopped in front of her and smiled down as he tugged the coil of hair resting on her shoulder. "I thought I wouldn't make it when the dog on the corner began to bark."

"Sampson's a big hound of some sort. He always frightens me."

"A hunting dog, well, that makes sense. Sampson caught my scent as I turned into the alley." He ran the palms of his hands down her arms. "But it was worth it to see your smile."

Margaret leaned against him and tipped her head back, hoping he would kiss her.

Instead, Ayden wrapped his arms around her and held her close. "I know it's dangerous for us to meet like this, but when I look into the fire, all I see is you."

"Truly?" Margaret pressed her cheek to his chest. "When I look into my heart, I find no one but you."

The silence stretched as they held each other, and Margaret blinked happy tears that threatened to spill from her eyes.

Ayden cleared his throat, sniffed, and then spoke, "This doesn't look like the same place. How did you manage so much in only a week?"

Margaret turned to gaze at her work with new eyes. She had transformed the dark and dusty playroom into a warm and welcoming hideaway.

A storage area in the basement of her home, packed with items destined for the less fortunate, provided material for her endeavor. Gayly patterned cloth, repurposed with her sewing skill, supplied curtains for the paper-covered windows. Cushions and a matching tablecloth graced the table and chairs, along with fresh-cut flowers as a centerpiece.

She'd found a folding camp bed to hold the mattress in the unused carriage area next door and secured sheets and covers from her linens at home. No longer a child's play-cushion on the floor, the tidy bed boasted a small night-stand that gleamed with new polish in the light of the covered oil lamp.

The coal stove filled with old ash had been cleaned and now held fresh kindling and waited for colder days to warm the tiny home.

"It turned out rather well if I do say so myself." She grinned up at him impishly. "You must appreciate how hard I worked to secure our comfort."

"Oh, I do, I do." He turned slowly, taking in all the changes in the small abode. "You are a most talented homemaker, Miss James."

Margaret responded with a dignified nod and a giggle. "You are quite welcome, Mr. MacKenna. Please, have a seat. Tell me how you've been. Until you surprised me last week, I hadn't seen you for a couple of years."

"Two years, seven months." Ayden pulled the chair that held his coat away from the small table and took a seat. "No big changes in my life, except the job at Murphy's Dry Goods. I clerk and clean for Mr. Murphy, load wagons and such." He laid his arm across the table, palm up and open, an invitation.

Margaret took his hand as she sat across the table from him.

"Oh! I do have one bit of surprising news. I'm going to have a sibling." His smile, always so engaging, grew wider, and his eyes shone with excitement. "I just found out last week."

"That's wonderful! I forget your parents are a great deal younger than mine." Her smile faltered as she thought of her father. "My mother was forty-one when I was born."

"My mother was a mere child of sixteen when she gave birth to me." His gaze rose from their clasped hands to her face. "They married when she was but fourteen."

"Can you imagine being married so young?"

"Actually," his eyes stared thoughtfully into hers, "I can."

Margaret's face heated despite the cool room. "I'll be fifteen in September," she murmured.

"I know." He lifted her hand and wove their fingers together, palm to palm. Jitters erupted in her stomach, and she looked away.

Finally, Ayden spoke, breaking the silence. "You haven't been to a coven meeting in years."

"I know." Margaret nodded and stared at their linked fingers. "Mother told me I'd not be allowed to join the coven, so there's no reason to accompany my brothers to the gatherings."

"Why not? Your mother's a member."

Margaret lifted one shoulder. "I think it has to do with what my brother told me. After the initiation ceremony, Bayard said that Leader Brown took him aside and had him swear an oath to the coven. One of the things he swore was never to wed an unskilled person."

Her gaze lifted from their hands to find him watching her. "My mother says she'll find a match for me and doesn't want her choices limited to coven members."

"A match?" Ayden released her hand and rose to pace away from the table. "Then you are to wed?" he spoke over his shoulder.

"Eventually, yes." Margaret came to her feet and took a hesitant step toward his broad back. "Mother presented me at a tea to the mothers and daughters of the Brahmin eight months ago, and I am of the age to have gentlemen callers—"

"You have suitors?" Ayden turned to her. Fear and disappointment played across his face. In a stilted voice, he inquired, "Are there any—*gentlemen callers*—you particularly admire?"

"What? Of course not." Determined not to allow a misunderstanding to fester between them, she crossed the distance and took his hand. "There is only one man I admire, and he stands before me. But what of you? You're the one who must marry within the coven."

A sigh released the tension in his shoulders, and he ran the knuckles of his free hand lovingly down her cheek and smiled. "We are safe there. The oath only requires I marry a woman skilled in elemental magic. And that, I most certainly intend to do."

"You have someone in mind?" She pulled her hand from his to step back, but he stopped her.

Large, calloused hands gently gripped her shoulders as he held her at arms-length.

She raised her head to see his expressive eyes and gauge his response. "Who do you intend to marry?"

His smile widened, and he arched one eyebrow at her. "Someday, I intend to wed the elemental witch who stands before me."

"Oh, Ayden!" Margaret returned to his arms and nestled her face against his shirt. "I liked you from the first day we met. Do you remember?"

"I certainly do." He ran his hands up and down her back and cuddled her close. "I had seen you in the flame the week before, running across a yard—a strange little girl—determination in her eyes. Then, at the gathering, when you raced toward me, I remembered the vision I'd seen in the fire."

"Your pyromancy."

"Yes. But that was the first vision I ever had that became a reality. I was speechless. Giddy with wonder. And you, the girl I had only seen in the fire, stood before me, grinning, with the ribbons falling from your hair."

"I don't sound very glamourous."

"We were children—and for me, it was momentous."

Margaret nodded her head against his chest.

It had been a momentous day for her as well. The first time she set eyes on Ayden and the last time she spoke to her father was on the same day.

That's the reason mother hates him so.

After several moments, Ayden ran his hands up and down her back then stepped away from their embrace. "I open the store in the morning. I need to go home and get some rest."

"You're leaving? Already?"

"We'll meet again—as often as you like." He retrieved his jacket and spun it over his head, slipping it on in the same motion. "Next time, we shall choose an evening where I don't work the next morning."

"I understand." She straightened his lapel and tipped her head back. "But you must kiss me farewell, for I shall think of nothing but you until we meet again."

"Oh, I must? Very well."

His lips, at first gentle, became more demanding. Margaret responded with an urgency she didn't quite understand. She wrapped her arms around his neck as their tongues danced a sensuous waltz between their lips.

Ayden pulled her body tight to his and ground a strange lump into her stomach. He groaned, then broke their deep kiss with a sudden gasp. "I must go, Margaret," he said breathlessly.

In the dim light, she found the swelling which strained against his trousers. Understanding made her blink, and she flushed with pleasure that a man, especially this man, found her desirable, followed quickly by concern that his unfulfilled lust might force him to seek elsewhere for release.

A dilemma she never considered before this moment.

Ayden bowed quickly from the room and closed the door.

She listened for the soft sound of the gate latch and knew he had gone. Now she had only to return to the house and her room without being seen.

She surveyed the carriage apartment for any telltale sign of their meeting and found none. The place was undisturbed except for her improvements. Satisfied, she extinguished the lanterns with a thought and slipped out into the early morning darkness.

Chapter 11

Ayden MacKenna

—

November 14, 1845 – Near Boston Harbor

Ayden placed the stack of blankets in the back of his family's wagon as he considered his most recent meeting with Margaret. Over the summer, their relationship had blossomed, and he knew without a doubt how much he loved her. However, every rendezvous required more restraint to refrain from doing what the images in the fire continued to proclaim they would soon do.

He put thoughts of Margaret's sweet kisses away and trudged the familiar walkway up to his family's small house. One last item for their journey waited beside the door.

Inside, his parents argued.

Not wishing to incur his mother's ire, he hesitated to enter.

More than annoyed, his mother embodied fury. "You will not treat me like an invalid, Lyam. I'm pregnant, not ill."

"Rachael," his father coaxed, "You're to deliver in a fortnight. We should stay at home."

"I told you, I need to receive a blessing for this birth, and I intend to do so at the coven meeting tonight. The Lord and Lady will certainly listen to a request made from the circle."

"The Lady will listen to us right here, sweetheart."

"Urgh! We've finished this discussion." Large-bellied and awkward, she marched through the door. "What are you smiling about?" She shot an angry look at Ayden.

He picked up the wicker basket and escorted her to the vehicle. "The wagon is ready." He set the basket on the bed of the wagon and the gave blankets an inviting pat. "We have soft blankets, pillows, and food for the trip."

"It is a four-hour ride, for heaven's sake, not a cross-country venture," his mother snapped.

Ayden and his father shared a look.

His mother passed him and pointed to the high seat. "Help me up."

"I thought you'd be more comfortable in the back." Ayden laced his fingers for a step, and his father steadied her from behind until she reached the seat.

"Perhaps later. For now, I want to see the road." She arranged her long coat over her legs and adjusted her warm hat. "Otherwise, I may feel ill."

Although the sky remained clear, Ayden sensed a disturbance building to the northwest. He climbed into the back of the wagon and covered his legs with one of the woolen blankets and scanned the sky. He'd learned he often failed to predict the weather and hoped he was only feeling anxious this time.

He looked forward to each coven moon and participating in the group worship of his Lord and Lady. Although he always wished Margaret could be there, it no longer mattered quite as much. They'd met several times over the summer and planned to meet again early next month.

As they made their way out of the city and southwest to Brown's farm, Ayden snuggled down into the straw. He tasted his top lip while reminiscing about his last rendezvous with Margaret. Their kisses, at first awkward and tentative, changed to passionate and lingering as the evening progressed.

"Ayden!"

His father's sharp tone woke Ayden from his dream. "I'm sorry, what?"

"Answer your mother, son."

Ayden looked at his mother's pale face. "Mum?"

She shook her head. "It's all right, Ayden. I just asked if I could rest in the back for a while. My back is aching."

They were far enough out of town that no traffic passed on the road. Lyam pulled the horse to a halt, and Ayden vaulted over the side of the wagon, then lowered the back brace. By the time he reached his mother, Lyam had already helped her to the ground.

"I'm fine, my love. I only want to lay down and stretch my back."

"We should have stayed home."

"Why does where I'm at make such a difference?"

The men steadied Rachael as she climbed into the back of the wagon.

"Because there are midwives and doctors in the city."

"None of which we can afford. Besides, I'm a midwife. I know what to expect and what to do."

"And you'll likely not be in a position to use your knowledge."

"Lyam, let me be." She seated herself on several blankets and arched her back, grimacing with pain.

Ayden jumped into the back beside his mother. He covered her with the extra blanket and tucked a pillow behind her shoulders. He settled beside her and nodded to his father to raise the back closure. "Are you more comfortable?"

"I think so. Yes." Her pale face twisted momentarily, then she opened her eyes and gave him an encouraging smile. "It will pass."

"Should we return home?" Ayden looked to his father.

Lyam shook his head. "We are closer to Garrett's. You slept for quite some time." He shook the reins, and the wagon lurched into motion.

When they reached the farmhouse, Lyam drove the wagon to the front steps of the house.

Once they stopped moving, Ayden helped his mother to her feet, then assisted her down into his father's waiting arms.

"Has the pain lessened?" Lyam asked.

Ayden scooped up the blankets and followed his parents into the house.

Inside, Garrett showed his parents to the main floor bedroom. "You can rest in here."

"I'm fine. You are all making too much of a fuss."

"Thank you," Lyam said over his shoulder to Garrett as he ushered his wife into the room.

Ayden placed the stack of blankets on a chair beside the bed. "I'll see to the wagon." Not sure if either parent heard him, he greeted Garrett, then headed outside.

Ayden guided the horse out of the circle drive and halted near the edge of the cleared field. He set the brake, then jumped down from the seat and covered the back of the wagon with an oilskin cloth. He unhitched the horse and walked the animal to Garrett's large corral behind the small barn.

One of Margaret's brothers forked hay into the feed trough. He looked up and grinned as Ayden led the pony into the enclosure.

"It's always good to see Jack is doing well." He indicated Ayden's horse then continued to fill the feed bin.

This must be Bayard.

Ayden couldn't tell the twins apart until they spoke. Friendly and engaging, Bayard was the exact opposite of his brother Bernard.

"That's right. Jack was yours. The old boy is getting on in years." Ayden removed the lead.

Jack approached Bayard and nosed his open hand, then poked his nostrils against his coat pocket.

"He remembers you." Ayden smiled at Bayard's delighted grin.

"There's a good boy." Bayard patted the gelding's neck and pulled a carrot from his pocket.

"How long have you been here?" Ayden asked.

Bayard chuckled at the horse, then grinned at Ayden, leaning his arm on the pitchfork handle. "About an hour, I'd guess. Bernard is preparing the pentacle for tonight's ceremony."

Ayden glanced up at the partially clouded sky. "We'll have snow by morning."

"I think so too." Bayard winked at Ayden. "It's a good thing Margaret stayed home with mother."

Ayden arched his brow. "I didn't want to ask."

"And now you don't have to."

They walked together around the barn and across the backyard. A fire burned in the outside pit, where one of the older children turned the long spit that held four chickens.

"Did you come to the meeting alone?" Bayard asked in the kitchen.

"No, with my parents."

Bayard tipped his head in surprise. "I thought you'd have a brother or sister by now, and your parents would be home with a baby."

Ayden shook his head. "She insisted on coming. She wants the coven to ask for a blessing for the birth."

"There you are!" Bernard half-shouted at his twin as he walked into the kitchen. "I needed you in the shelter."

"I know, but I was occupied as well." Bayard offered his brother his cup of cider.

"I still need your help." Bernard ignored the drink and stalked out the door.

Bayard finished his drink and set the cup on the counter. "May the Lady protect your mother," he said, then followed his twin from the house.

When dinner was ready, his mother ate with the rest of the coven members in Garrett's living area. She spoke with several of the women members before returning to the bedroom to lie down.

As the time approached for the moon ceremony, most of the members in the farmhouse departed, robes in hand, for the large barn. Two of the women chose to remain with Rachael—just in case she needed help.

Ayden and his father exchanged worried frowns. "Are you going to the meeting?" Ayden asked.

"Your mother wants me to ask the Lady's blessing for this birth." He shook his head and lowered his voice. "She didn't act this way when you were born. I fear there may be something wrong—something she hasn't shared with me."

Ayden's heart contracted, and an ugly weight settled in his stomach. "I'll stay here with mum."

Lyam gripped Ayden's shoulder, then withdrew his robe from their bags that rested in the corner and followed Garrett out the door.

Ayden paced the room.

As the night stretched long into the morning, it was clear a birth was imminent. The women who stayed with his mother sent him to fetch towels, extra bedding, and water, both hot and cool. Whenever he tried to peek into the room, the door was unceremoniously closed in his face.

He stopped several times to stare into the flames.

Show me mother five years from now.

But the fire failed to show him anything at all.

Show me my brother.

A swirling coalescence crystalized into a face just beyond the flame. A chubby laughing toddler wobbled across their front room on the north side. His smiling father capturing the baby before the child fell as he turned with a laugh to look at—who?

The door burst open, ending his vision. His father swept through the door tracking snow and cold into the room. "Anything?"

Ayden shook his head just as a baby's sharp cry sounded beyond the closed bedroom door.

"Rachael?" his father shouted and rushed toward the birthing room as the door opened.

One of the women smiled from the doorway, holding a swaddled child. "Congratulations, Lyam. You have a son." The woman pushed the baby into Lyam's arms. "Your wife is fine, but you must let us clean up a bit before you see her."

The bedroom door closed again.

Lyam turned to the growing group of coven members coming in out of the cold and lifted the child in his arms. "It's a boy!"

Ayden glanced out the window. Snow piled against the glass and obscured his view of the yard.

The women with his mother called for more bedding and warm water. After consulting with Garrett, the leader searched a trunk in his attic, obtaining more bedding. It took over an hour before the women deemed it suitable for the men to enter the birth chamber.

By then, the crowd of coven members had disbursed. Nearby neighbors hitched their wagons and returned home. Many that had traveled camped inside the big barn or took lodging in the bedrooms upstairs.

As usual, Garrett gave up his room to a coven family and made his bed before the fire in the living room.

Ayden thought they would all sleep as a family in the bedroom. His father, in bed with his mother, with him, on the floor near the fire.

The women who helped his mother dissuaded him of this idea immediately.

"We will stay with your mother tonight, and as long as she needs the help of womanly hands," the oldest of the pair told them as they entered the room. "Visit for a few moments, then let your wife rest. It was a difficult birth."

A difficult birth.

Ayden swallowed and followed his father into the room. The bedroom was warm, almost hot, as the fire burned cheerfully in the fireplace. Lanterns were turned low, and the shutters closed against the night. His mother looked up and smiled as they approached the bed.

"My love." She reached for Lyam's hand. Her other arm clasped firmly around the baby at her breast. "Ayden. You were both right. We should have stayed home."

"Perhaps," Lyam kissed her hand. "But you had help here you wouldn't have had at home, and prayers from the entire coven beseeching the Lady's blessing, which I'm sure she bestowed. All is well."

"All is well," Rachael echoed.

Her skin appeared translucent to Ayden. Delicate and thin. Dark circles rimmed her sunken red eyes. Still, when she smiled at him, he smiled back.

She needs time to recover. It was a difficult birth.

"Have you decided on a name?" Ayden asked. To his ears, he sounded a stranger.

"Melvyn," his mother replied and grinned at his father. "M-e-l-v-y-n. Melvyn MacKenna."

"After my father," Lyam murmured.

"Yes. I thought you'd approve."

"I do."

"Do you want to hold your son?"

Baby Melvyn had released his mother's nipple and slept soundly, milk clinging to his tiny lips.

"No. I'll wake him."

"I doubt that. He sleeps well for being so tiny."

"Holding your son will have to wait, I'm afraid." The coven ladies had returned. "Your wife needs to rest, and so do you two. There'll be plenty of time to hold this lad in the days to come." The older lady plucked Melvyn from his mother's arms and covered Rachael's exposed nipple with one deft movement. She handed the baby to the younger woman and pointed to the rocking chair.

"Now off you both go. Say good night to your wife and find a place to sleep in front of the fire with Leader Brown."

"Goodnight," Ayden said, uneasy with the pallor on his mother's face.

Lyam kissed his wife's brow and whispered in her ear, then the two of them returned to the main room, the door closed firmly behind them.

Garrett sat on the floor, leaning against the old sofa, smoking a pipe. Three stacks of blankets and pillows beside him. He grinned as the two men approached.

"Is baby and mama doing well?"

"Yes." Lyam lowered himself to the floor across from Garrett. "But we may be staying for a while longer than we originally planned."

"I should think so." Garrett chuckled and emptied his pipe near the embers. "I don't think you'll be heading home for a week at least, but that's my guess."

"I should return to Boston." Ayden hung his head. "Mr. Murphy depends on me to take care of the books and fill orders." He met his father's gaze. "But if you think you need me here—"

"No, no. You should go home. I need you to speak with the owners where I work. Ask for Mr. Hawsey or Mr. Freid. Let them know about your mother. Tell them a week, maybe more, before Rachael can travel."

"I will."

"You might ride back to Boston with the James twins," Garrett suggested. "They'll leave in the morning. Also, the Warren and Roberta Johnson live in town."

"I'll find a way back." Ayden arranged his blankets before the fire and lay down staring into the embers until his eyes closed, listening to his father and Garrett speak of mundane things.

Melvyn woke them twice during the night, and an early morning flurry of activity with the women needing more towels ended any chance for Ayden to return to sleep. He set a large pot of water boiling over the firepit outside, then went in search of a ride home.

In the end, he left the farm midday with the Johnsons.

Warren and Rachael were only a year older than Ayden. He had apprenticed with a cobbler, and his wife helped instruct children at a nearby school. They lived with Warren's older brother Wrigley.

The snow lay on the ground and clung to the trees. Last night's storm ushered in cold clear skies and freezing temperatures. Ayden shivered so much on the ride back home he thought he might have worn blisters on his frozen rear-end.

The Johnson's dropped Ayden off close to Murphy's Dry Goods. He walked the rest of the way, stopping at the farrier's where his father worked to tell Mr. Hawsey, the owner, the news.

Mr. Hawsey was pleased to hear Lyam had another son but unhappy he would be away from work for so long.

"I don't have to tell you there's shoeing to be done. Schedules will need to be changed, and customers will be unhappy," Hawsey grumbled.

"I'm sure my father has this in mind and will be back as soon as my mother can travel."

"It'd best be soon." Mr. Hawsey stalked away and disappeared into a back room.

The dark and cold rooms at home matched his mood. Ayden lit a fire in the stove and rested his head in his hands. Hesitantly, he opened the door on the stove and stared into the fire.

"Show me, my mother," he commanded, guiding his vision with the skill he'd acquired over the years. Immediately, a scene resolved to reveal his mother resting in her bed at home, his father by her side.

I could have lost her.

Although his mother said nothing, Ayden believed her healing skill had kept her alive during the difficult birth. Still, in her weakened condition, she would need care.

Father could lose his job.

What would they do then? He'd be more than willing to give his parents his earnings and what he had saved, but he knew they would discourage his charity.

I have a brother.

Wonder spread through his chest, and he inhaled deeply. He'd never thought to have a sibling. *Elemental magic* offered much, but it took away the bounty of a large family. More than one child was rare.

Except for the James family.

Immediately, Margaret's face, alight with a smile, filled the flames. Before his lack of good sense took hold, he closed the stove door.

I must work in the morning.

He would wait to tell her the news about his baby brother when they met at the end of the week. Of course, her brothers would have already shared the information. With a disappointed sigh, he reached over and opened the stove door.

Immediately, Margaret's face appeared and became smaller as the scene expanded. Clad in only his shirt, she leaned her hip against the small counter in the carriage apartment.

Besides the obvious, I wish I knew what this meant.

This encounter between them replayed so often in the fire it must have some hidden meaning.

Like all the times he'd watched this unfold before, Margaret pushed her tangled hair back from her face and shook her head at him. With a chuckle, she stepped forward into his arms. "Don't worry so much. Everything will be all right." Her hand caressed the side of his face as she gazed into his eyes. "I love you so much."

The vision ended with his head lowering to capture her lips as her lashes fluttered closed.

Chapter 12

Margaret James

—

June 1847 – Beacon Hill

Margaret clipped on the second pearl earring and turned to view both adornments in the reflection to ensure she placed them evenly.

Good enough.

Her mother had informed her at breakfast that she and Margaret would host a tea this afternoon for a few dear acquaintances.

I wasn't aware my mother had any dear acquaintances.

Margaret backed from the mirror and turned from side to side to view her dress. The bell of the tan silk skirt accented the curve at her waist. The wide neckline, which rested at the edge of her shoulders, was daringly fashionable yet appropriate for afternoon tea.

Curious about the guests downstairs, she dismissed the lady's maid and hurried from her room. Voices from the sitting room echoed up the staircase as she descended.

A man and a woman visitor from the sound of it. Likely, another gentleman and his mother.

Chantal's efforts to wed her daughter were becoming obvious and increasingly tedious. However, these were the first visitors to be classified as '*dear acquaintances.*'

Annoyed yet intrigued, Margaret paused at the sitting room doorway. The female visitor had already taken her seat, and her mother's full skirt blocked the woman's identity.

His back to the door, Margaret had the impression the gentleman wore a type of uniform.

He had yet to remove his cap or his frock-length tailored jacket. Pleated at the waist, the hem of his coat swayed above tall black boots as he spoke to Margaret's mother. Golden buttons adorned the oversized cuffs allowing only a hint of white shirtsleeve to contrast the tan skin of his hands. Familiarity tickled the back of her mind.

Do I know him?

"Please come in, Margaret. No need to peek around the doorway." Chantal's smile took the sting from her words as she held her skirt and took a seat in the room's only other single chair, which left the settee for Margaret and their male guest.

The man spun toward the doorway and smiled. "My God, it's good to see you again."

"Robert!" Propriety forgotten, Margaret took two steps into the room and flung her arms around his neck. "I've missed you so. I thought you'd never return."

Robert lifted Margaret from her feet and turned in a circle, reminiscent of their childhood games. "I've only been away for a few years." He set her down and took her hands. "Unfortunately, this is but a brief visit home while father commissions the newest ship into our fleet. We've six vessels now." He removed his narrow-brimmed Mariner's cap and followed her to the settee and sat beside her. "Once the crew is secured, I will depart again as the First Mate on the new ship – *Wayfarer's Dawn*."

"How exciting." Margaret clasped his calloused hand with her own. "Congratulations!" In the two years they were apart, he had grown at least six inches and had matured into a man's physique.

No wonder I didn't recognize him.

"Perhaps Robert would like to escort you for a walk in the park before the heat of the day advances." Her mother handed Robert's pale and thin mother a cup of tea. "Agatha and I have a great deal to discuss." She raised an eyebrow at Robert and gave Margaret a satisfied smirk.

Eager to escape her mother's obvious matchmaking, Margaret stood and brushed her skirt. "Yes. Let's." She held out her hand to Robert, led him to the foyer, and chose one of the parasols from the umbrella stand near the door. Once outside, she marched down the front steps to the street as though to outrun her overbearing mother.

"Ho there, slow down." Robert kept pace as they crossed the cobbled street and proceeded down the walkway toward the park. "I've never known you to run from a fight."

"There is no fight, not with mother. She presses and coerces until everyone around her simply gives in."

"Except you."

Margaret stopped at the corner and opened her parasol. "It's true. I become stubborn, and we argue. Her latest insistence is that I become betrothed." They continued toward the park at a reduced pace. "The parade of eligible suitors never seems to end."

"And is there no suitor you find attractive?" Amusement colored his tone.

"None of which my mother would approve." Margaret looked up in time to catch his smile. "What of you? No one has caught your eye?"

"I have been on a ship traveling the world, or have you forgotten?"

They bumped together companionably as they strolled, and she took his arm. "I know. I feel your absence wholeheartedly. You are forever my one true friend."

"And you, mine." He laid his hand over her fingers wrapped on the inside of his elbow. "Honestly, I doubt I shall ever marry. Although, when I'm asked about someone special waiting for me at home, I tell them about you. I hope you don't mind."

They reached the park entrance and turned onto the cobbled promenade that wove through the greenery.

"Of course not. I'm sincerely flattered."

"Good." Robert tipped his cap at a couple that passed them on the walkway. "I did notice you've practiced your homemaking skills in our playhouse."

Her breath caught, and her face warmed. "You went to the carriage apartment?"

"First thing when I got home. I hold the memory of playing dolls there with you close to my heart." He stepped off the path and halted near a bench beneath the shade of a large elm. "At first, the changes shocked me. But I recognized the handiwork as yours, and after the surprise diminished, I saw what a lovely hideaway you had made."

Margaret swallowed, hoping to find a drop of moisture for her throat. "I-uh. I hope you're not upset."

"Heavens, no." He led her to the narrow bench and placed his handkerchief on the seat to not soil her skirt with dampness. "Sometimes, it's nice to get away to a place with no expectations—where you can be completely yourself—even if it is only a small carriage apartment."

"Yes, it is," Margaret agreed as she closed her parasol. She held her face steady as panic set in. In the excitement of seeing Robert again, her rendezvous tonight with Ayden had slipped from her mind.

I must warn him not to come.

But how?

He cannot come to the apartment until Robert sets sail.

The heady scent of roses drifted by on the summer air, and an occasional puffy cloud crossed the clear blue sky.

Robert stretched his long legs out in front of him and closed his eyes with a sigh. "This is what I dream of when I dream of home." He lifted his face to the breeze and inhaled deeply. "Sitting on a summer's day talking with you."

Margaret chewed the side of her cheek with worry.

The silence between them grew, broken occasionally by the greeting of strollers passing by.

"Do you think they've planned our wedding yet?" Robert queried.

"Oh, no doubt." Margaret summoned a small chuckle and looked over at him. "Along with the names of our children."

Robert laughed aloud, and several people looked their way. "Perhaps we should return before they decry your reputation ruined and force the issue of our marriage."

"Yes, I believe we should." She took his arm, and they returned the way they had come.

Once home, Margaret replaced the parasol in the umbrella stand beside the door, preceded Robert to the sitting room, and halted. Their mothers were absent, and the seating area tidied.

"I wonder where they've gone?" Robert murmured. "Mother isn't well enough to go out. She wouldn't have come today if father hadn't insisted."

"Her nurse saw her home," Chantal spoke as she descended the staircase. "She wasn't feeling well, and we didn't know when you two would come back." She beamed at the young couple, then continued into the dining room. "If you would like tea, I could have some brought in."

"No, thank you." Robert backed toward the front door. "I need to return home and check on mother. It was a pleasure seeing you again, Mrs. James," to Margaret, he added, "I won't sail without seeing you again."

"How long before you go?"

"At least a week, perhaps two. Not long, I'm afraid." He took her hand, then leaned forward to kiss her cheek.

Margaret tightened her grip on his hands and then released him. "I hope your mother begins to feel better."

"Thank you." Robert touched the brim of his hat, tipped it to Chantal, then opened the door and departed.

"I must say, little Robert Prescott has grown into a fine man," Chantal remarked, her gaze on Margaret's flushed face.

"He has indeed." Her mother's opinion of Robert was of little concern to Margaret at that moment. She had to find a way to warn Ayden not to go to the carriage apartment for two weeks, perhaps three, to be safe. "I just remembered; I must order a new pair of gloves. My beige thread pair are soiled."

"Oh Margaret, your allowance on gloves is through the roof. How do they keep getting stained?"

"That remains a mystery." Margaret shrugged. "Could you ask for the carriage to be brought 'round front? I'll fetch my clutch."

Chantal huffed in annoyance but pulled the bell chord by the dining room door. "Very well—if you must. My maid can accompany you."

"No need," Margaret called down the stairs. "The driver will be enough. There will be no packages to carry." She snatched her beaded reticule from her the bureau in her room and hurried back down the stairs.

Her mother waited at the door. "Are you certain this is necessary? I doubt Robert would mind a stain on your gloves. He knows how you are, after all."

"I'll mind, mother." Margaret selected the same parasol and opened the door. "I won't be gone long."

In only a few moments, the family carriage rounded the corner and halted at the front step.

The driver, acting as a footman, jumped down to assist Margaret into the carriage.

"Thank you, uh-er—"

"Elmont, Miss James."

"Thank you, Elmont." Margaret held his arm as she climbed into the carriage. "I need to stop at the glovers on Hanover, then on to a Murphy's Mercantile off Charter Street. Do you know where that is?"

"Yes, Miss." Elmont closed the carriage door.

The vehicle leaned as it took the driver's weight, then pitched into motion.

Margaret raised the window shade to watch the residential lane change to city streets. She could have easily walked to the glover. The milliner, glover, and seamstress were located just north of the residence, a few blocks away. The mercantile where Ayden worked would be further north, near the docks. She had no business on the north docks and hoped Elmont would hold his tongue.

I can't count on that.

She'd have to come up with a reason, but at this moment, her ride across town felt so fraught with possible calamities, and she couldn't think of a single thing.

Her hand size, noted on the family account, made the visit to the glover straightforward and routine. In short order, she returned to the street where the vehicle waited.

"Now to the mercantile," she instructed as Elmont assisted her into the carriage.

"Yes, miss."

Although they often talked of it, she'd never been to Ayden's place of employment, but she knew the location. She wouldn't have dreamed of intruding there at any other time but couldn't risk Ayden's discovery by Robert or his father and facing accusations of trespassing or worse.

The pedestrians outside the window changed from businessmen and fashionable ladies to sailors and families with small children looking lost in the big city.

Immigrants, most likely.

She sent up a prayer to the Lord and Lady for their wellbeing.

The carriage slowed and pulled out of traffic just as Murphy's Dry Goods came into view. The vehicle halted, and in moments Elmont opened the door.

"Miss?"

Margaret smiled apologetically at the driver and descended from the carriage. "I shouldn't be too long."

Another carriage passed by, squeezing between the James carriage and the raised wooden walkway in front of the shops. He made a rude gesture at them.

"I believe I should move the carriage." Elmont watched the disrespectful driver round the corner. "I've been in this part of town before. There's a livery stable with space for carriages right 'round the corner—toward the harbor."

"That's fine. Find yourself some lunch as well and meet me back here in an hour."

"Oh, I couldn't leave you alone, Miss James."

"I won't be alone. I'll be in the shop." She pointed across the street. "If I need you, I'm sure they have message runners." As she finished speaking, a young boy with a knit cap rushed out of Murphy's with a note in his hand and made a mad dash down the street.

Margaret opened her parasol, signaling the end of the conversation, and crossed the narrow lane to the store.

A bell above the door announced her arrival.

She closed her parasol and paused to compose herself as she looked over the store. Shelves lined the walls from floor to ceiling, filled with everything from cooking pots to grocery items. Bolts of cloth filled a bin to her right in a colorful display of new fabric. The shop smelled a mixture of coffee, tobacco, and cinnamon.

"One moment, please. I'll be right with you." A gangly youth, all arms and legs, descended a ladder near the back of the store. He wiped his hands on his apron and smiled. "What can I help you find?"

"I'm looking for Ayden MacKenna. Is he available?"

"Certainly. Let me fetch him for you." The young man rounded the long empty table with measuring marks etched on it, stepped into an open door behind the counter, and called, "Ayden! Someone is asking for you." He turned his smile on Margaret. "He'll be down in two shakes."

"Thank you." Drawn to the material display, Margaret pulled off her glove and ran her fingertips over the different textures of each bolt of fabric. Along the far wall, a collection of clocks struck the hour of twelve. She drew the glove back onto her hand.

"Hello?" Ayden called over the chimes. "How may I help you?"

Margaret rounded the aisle, and their gazes met.

His brow rose in astonishment, and he glanced over his shoulder before he spoke. "What a lovely surprise."

"I need a moment of your time," her voice lowered when she saw the youth watching them from behind the counter. "Can you take a break for lunch?"

"Excellent idea." He turned to the worker. "Gilbert, I'm going out for lunch. Please let Mr. Murphy know." To Margaret, he said, "Allow me to retrieve my hat."

The store clerk bobbed his head as Ayden returned to the back room. "I will, if he asks," the clerk called to Ayden's back when he returned to Margaret.

Ayden opened the door and ushered her onto the boardwalk.

Margaret opened her parasol. "Where shall we go?"

"There's a hotel a block up with an eatery at the entrance." He grinned. "Very respectable. Mr. Murphy and his wife dine there on occasion."

"I can't be long. My driver will look for me in an hour." She glanced up at his beaming face. "You can't come to the apartment tonight. The family is home for a few weeks."

He slowed to a stop on the boardwalk. "That *is* disappointing." He pointed out the hotel's open double doors. "Let's find a seat, and we can talk."

Margaret closed her parasol and entered the establishment. She stopped inside, unsure how to proceed, as no host or hostess greeted her.

"This way." Ayden wove his way around tables, half of which were unoccupied, to the back of the small space and pulled out a chair for Margaret. "How is this?"

She followed his path, noticing both dock workers and businessmen enjoying their lunch. "This will be fine."

Ayden hung his hat on one of the pegs beside the table. "Your parasol?"

"Yes, please." Unlooping the wrist ribbon, she passed it to Ayden.

Seated, he faced the café entrance while Margaret faced a hallway leading to the kitchen and the hotel lobby beyond.

The café filled quickly with the lunch crowd.

"They have a delicious clam soup, served with freshly baked bread. It is the house specialty and served quickly."

"That will be fine. I'd also like a cup of tea."

Ayden waved a waitress to their table. "Two soups with bread and tea."

The waitress nodded her understanding and carried her tray of empty dishes into the kitchen area.

"So, your friend and her father have returned home?"

"My friend and *his* father, and yes. They are acquiring a new ship, and his mother has been ill."

"I was under the mistaken impression your childhood friend was female."

"I know, and I did not dissuade you of the notion. But my friend is a male and will set sail on the new ship in their fleet in a few weeks. Once father and son have departed, we can safely resume our meetings."

"I see."

The waitress brought their meal and moved on.

Margaret tasted the soup and was pleasantly surprised by the texture and the taste. It rivaled anything their cook at home could make. "This is delicious."

"Yes, it is," Ayden agreed. "It's one of the reasons this establishment is so popular."

After consuming most of his chowder, Ayden set his spoon aside. "I take it you haven't told your good friend about us."

Margaret dabbed her mouth with her napkin and shook her head. "I have not, nor do I intend to. I do not discuss my family's—*talents*—with Robert. And since you are a part of that world, I have never mentioned you to him."

"Has he noticed the changes to your playroom?"

"Yes. And Robert approves of my homemaking skills."

Ayden stared at his partially empty bowl for several seconds, his shoulders stiff with tension. "Is Robert one of your suitors?"

Margaret waited until he raised his gaze to hers. "Our families believe Robert and I would be a good pair. He and I discussed it and are firmly against the match. It is, however, practical for both of us to allow our parents to believe we are not opposed to the idea."

"I see," Ayden repeated himself. "How will I know when it's safe to meet again?"

Margaret placed her napkin beside her bowl. "Let's plan to meet three weeks from tonight. Robert felt certain they would set sail in two weeks."

"And if Robert doesn't sail in two weeks? How will I know to wait?" Ayden set the payment for their lunch on the table, then stood to hold Margaret's chair.

"I'm not sure. Coming back to the docks so soon would draw suspicion. Being here at all is cause for concern." Margaret opened her parasol as they stepped into the afternoon sunshine.

"How about this—Murphy's has recently received a shipment of rare tea from China. Take a small amount today as your reason for coming to the store. If Robert has not set sail in three weeks, send your driver to purchase another portion of tea. I'll know of the purchase and understand we must wait."

"Does no one else purchase this tea?"

"It was a special order. The customer declined to complete the transaction after the tea arrived. I have the canister in my office and will keep it on hold until our date has passed." Ayden opened the door to the dry goods store, and the bell rang overhead.

"I'll be right back with your tea."

The young worker was engaged with another customer, and Ayden disappeared into the back room.

Across the store, the clocks showed a quarter till the hour.

When Ayden returned, he handed her a folded envelope with *China Green Flower* written on the front.

"I must pay for this," Margaret insisted.

"This is only a sample portion. If you like it, you may purchase more." He winked and grinned.

Margaret put the envelope in her handbag. "I shall. Thank you for your understanding about this evening and the delicious lunch."

"You know you are always welcome." His voice dropped to a whisper.

The touch of his breath on her neck sent gooseflesh down her arm.

He held the door, and she opened her parasol on the walkway. "I'll be seeing you."

"Yes. Goodbye for now."

She hesitated, wanting to kiss him and touch his face, but the ridiculous notion passed, and she turned away. Two stores down, she spotted the James' carriage turning onto the street. She raised a gloved hand.

Elmont directed the carriage out of traffic and helped her into the coach. "Did you not find what you were looking for?"

"I did, and I purchased some exotic tea from China. I would say this has been a successful excursion."

"Very good, Miss James. Home now?"

"Yes, Elmont. Take us home."

Two weeks later, amidst the fourth of July celebration in Boston Harbor, Robert's ship, the *Wayfarer's Dawn*, set sail.

Margaret waved from the crowded dock until the ship rounded the bend in the harbor.

Smaller ships, decorated with patriotic flags, sailed across the water, making it difficult for the larger merchant vessels to navigate the channel. Still, after a few near mishaps, Robert was on his way.

After supper, the night before, Robert confided his father had given instructions to the doctor for how to handle burial arrangements for his mother should the worst happen while they were away. The family had discussed the men delaying their departure, but Agatha's condition could remain steady for years or decline overnight. In the end, they gave the doctor and his mother's nurse telegraph instructions for the ports they intended to visit and hoped to return within two years.

It was the best they felt they could do.

Bernard and Bayard had escorted Margaret and her mother to the docks to say farewell. The twins talked together in their disjointed way as they returned to the carriage.

"Raleigh?" Bayard asked.

"Before that," Bernard replied after several silent minutes.

I never know what they're talking about with half the conversation in their head.

The twins planned to leave that night on a trip south along the coast, which would take several weeks. Managing properties kept the pair busy and out of her hair. Therefore, they would be out of town when she met with Ayden. Getting in and out of the house was less worrisome with them gone.

She missed Ayden. Although she knew she loved Robert and always would, he didn't set her pulse on fire like Ayden.

Ayden.

Their kisses and petting strengthened her desire to be with him in every way. At nearly seventeen, she wanted the dream of marriage, and all it entailed, more than the restrictive benefits and wealth of Brahmin society afforded her.

She decided in the carriage on the ride home.

We have waited long enough.

Chapter 13

Ayden MacKenna

—

July 1847 – Near Boston Harbor

Ayden dried and stacked the last dinner plate in the cupboard. Outside, the summer sun beat down on the harbor city from a hot and hazy sky.

He draped the damp dishtowel over his shoulder and watched Melvyn nestle close to their mother despite the day's heat.

Seated together in an old, cushioned chair Garrett gave them, Rachael told her youngest a children's tale. His mother's pale face, thin and weary, smiled weakly at the two-year-old at her side. She paused and lifted her tired gaze to her eldest son. "I'd like to lie down a bit before dinner, sweetheart. Could you watch Mel until your father returns?"

"Of course! Consider me at your service." He wiped his hands again on the towel then tossed the well-worn cloth onto the counter. "Come here, little brother, ugh! You're getting so big."

Melvyn giggled as Ayden struggled to lift him from their mother's lap. He staggered away with Mel in his grip, then hoisted him to his hip. "Tell mama to have a nice nap."

"Nap-nap, mama." Melvyn waved at Rachael.

Rachael smiled at her sons, then drew the curtain that separated the seating area from the small alcove where his parents slept.

Ayden carried Mel outside and set him down in the empty garden patch near the front door.

The east side of their home provided an edge of shade from the late afternoon sun. Ayden sat on the step and watched Mel dig with an old broken spoon in the dirt.

"What are you making?"

"Dig."

"I see that." Ayden chuckled.

The afternoon's attempt at a breeze cooled the back of Ayden's neck, and he closed his eyes to enjoy the sensation.

Margaret's driver did not arrive at Murphy's to purchase or return the tea today, which meant her *dear friend* Robert and his father had sailed. Their rendezvous could go on as planned. The journey from his home to the carriage apartment had become routine over the last two years, and he always carried a small treat for the dog on the corner.

Keeping his mind off Margaret and her friend, Robert, frustrated Ayden. Several times over the last few weeks, he demanded the flame show him his rival, but it never had—only Margaret.

Margaret laughing at him, fully clothed, from the bed.

Margaret stalking him, half-dressed, around the small table, laughing at him.

Margaret crossing the short distance between them, wearing nothing but his shirt.

They would already be married if she were anyone else but Margaret James of the lauded Boston Brahmins.

Ayden glanced at the doorway of their small home near the northside docks and wondered.

How can I leave here to be with Margaret when my family needs me so?

"That's a sad look, son. What troubles you?" Lyam pushed freshly washed wet hair from his brow.

"Nothing really, just worried about mother." Ayden smiled a greeting at his father. "You stopped at a bathhouse on your way home."

"There's a new place to wash under the docks." He held up a roll of soiled clothing. "Fortunately, I remembered to bring a change of clothes this time.

Mucking stables is smelly work." He set the dirty garments near the neighbor's door. "This job pays me, *and I pay* the neighbor, Mrs. Corrigan." He shrugged and chuckled, then became serious. "How's your mother today?"

"Tired. She's laying down." Both men watched Melvyn dig. He had four small holes in the dirt and was busy excavating a fifth.

Lyam leaned close to Ayden. "You've stayed home at night these last few weeks. I thought perhaps the sadness I saw...," his voice trailed into silence, and then his brows rose in surprise. "You thought I didn't know."

"I—" Words failed, and he shook his head.

"I know you leave the house regularly after we've gone to bed and return before dawn." He reached down and lifted Melvyn from the ground. "You're a man fully grown, and I don't begrudge you a private life away from your family." He raised one brow and smiled at Ayden. "I remember being young. Having a drink with friends at a tavern. I thought perhaps one of the friendly young servers had caught your eye, then broke your heart."

"Umm."

"I don't ask for your confidence. A man's secrets are his own." His father opened the door with one hand, holding Mel secure with the other. "Your mother doesn't know of your late-night adventures, which is best. She would worry. But you don't have to crawl out the window. Just close the door quietly when you leave."

Alone on the stoop, Ayden ran his hand through his thick dark hair. He and Margaret had been meeting for over two years now, and his father never revealed he knew. That his father guessed he had a woman in town was understandable. His visions of Margaret at times left him in desperate need of female comfort, easily obtained at any of the dockside taverns. He tried not to seek his ease there, but there were times. There were times.

Ayden took a deep breath and looked down the block. A bath at the docks was a good idea. He'd have just enough time before the neighbor who did their laundry, Mrs. Corrigan, brought over their dinner. People on the poor side of Boston learned to lean on each other to make sure everyone got by.

Ayden stood and dusted his trousers, then headed toward the docks. His thoughts filled with Margaret and the anticipation of seeing her once again.

Near midnight, Ayden carefully closed his front door and hurried up the hill. The warmth of the hot summer day lingered in the humid night air. Perspiration quickly soaked his freshly laundered shirt.

Ayden tossed Sampson a chunk of roast chicken as he turned the corner into the alley behind Margaret's house. He hesitated at the gate and listened to the silence of the night before he lifted the metal latch and crept into the yard. In three long strides, he rounded the edge of the small structure and slipped inside the door.

With the windows closed and covered, the carriage apartment sweltered with near unbearable heat.

On the bed beside a shielded lantern, Margaret waited in the dusky glow of the screened light. She had partially undressed to accommodate the heat. Her slippers lay discarded in the corner, and her jacket hung over the back of the chair. She held her dark heavy hair from her neck as though she hoped to catch a breeze in the small, closed room. Damp tendrils clung to her neck, face, and shoulders. Her camisole, unlaced part-way down from the rounded neckline, had been untucked from her thin, cotton skirt and clung to her frame.

Margaret stood as he eased the door shut behind him. "Oh, Ayden!" She flung herself into his arms, kissing his neck and the side of his face. "I've missed you so."

The eerie sense he'd experienced this moment before filled his mind. The image from the flames, the scene he'd watched on a dozen occasions, merged with reality. Only this time, he could taste the sweetness and experience the softness of Margaret's mouth as their lips met.

Foreknowledge spoke to him and the tiny hairs on the back of his neck lifted.

It happens tonight.

Margaret clung to him. Her arms, at first around his neck, lowered to his shirt front. "Your shirt...it's drenched," she muttered between kisses. "Did it rain?"

"No." He moved forward as she stepped back toward the bed in a familiar dance. "I wish it would rain. It would be a relief."

"Take it off." Her fingers worked the buttons at his chest. "It will dry quicker."

He beat her to the last few buttons, then flung his shirt at the other chair.

Her fingers splayed across his chest, and she tipped her head back to look into his eyes. "I don't want to wait anymore. I'm tired of pretending I could ever love anyone but you."

"You know I feel the same. I'd wed you today—tonight if we could, but our families will never allow it."

"Then let's run away. Make a home for ourselves where no one knows who we are."

"I've always wanted to see New York."

The last step in their dance collided with the edge of the bed, and they tumbled onto the mattress, laughing.

His mouth found hers, and he slid his hand up her slick leg, past her knee, to her hip. He raised his head in astonishment. "This is new."

"It's too hot for drawers," Margaret murmured. She wrapped her legs around one of his and pressed herself against his thigh. A groan escaped her, and she squeezed his leg between hers. "Make me your wife, Ayden, if not in word, then in deed. I swear, I will never love another as I love you."

"And I, you." Ayden slipped his other hand beneath her camisole and caressed her back, damp with perspiration. The lacing, tight at her waist, hampered his reach. "Can this come off?" he asked, his voice breathless as he tugged at the material.

Margaret pushed him to the side and sat up. She gripped the edge of the camisole with crossed arms and drew it over her head. She tossed it across the room in one swift motion.

Once liberated from her chemise, nothing hampered his view. In the dim shine of the lamplight, her breasts glimmered with moisture, globes of living flesh.

Perfection.

"By the Goddess, you are so beautiful." Ayden's lips followed hers as she reclined back on the bed. His palm cradled the side of her breast while his thumb gently brushed the nipple.

Her mouth opened, and a soft sigh escaped her throat. "How that feels—I can't explain."

"Do you like it?"

Margaret's eager nod was all the encouragement he required.

His mouth left hers and trailed down her arched neck to her breasts which he cupped close together with both hands. He licked and suckled one tip and then the other.

Her thighs squeezed his thigh, and she pressed against him and moaned. "I never knew."

"There's more." Ayden kissed her side, tasting the saltiness of her hot skin as he made his way to her waist. He worked the clasp on the band of her skirt, then rose to his knees. "Lift your hips." When she complied, he pulled the material from beneath her and removed it from around her legs. He tossed the skirt over the chair that held her jacket.

In the shuttered light, her naked body shimmered with sweat. In all the flames Ayden had ever watched, he'd never seen this. Her arms relaxed above her head in a pillow of long dark hair. A triangle of curls the same color graced her body where her legs met. Her thighs parted slightly to either side of his knee. His gaze traveled back up her length and watched a small bead of perspiration slide from between her breasts down her side.

"What's the matter with me?" With a thought, the air inside the apartment stirred. A soft breeze cooled the moisture that covered them both.

"Ah," Margaret breathed with delight. "I should have thought of that. There's a beaker of water on the table."

"Thirsty?" Ayden's long reach spanned the distance, and he handed her the glass flask.

They both took a sip before Ayden returned the bottle to the table. As he turned back, Margaret sat up and kissed the small dark hairs that trailed down from his navel. She worked the top button on his breeches. "And these? Can they come off?"

He fought against the urgent desire her fingers kindled as she slowly worked the top clasp. "Here, let me."

Margaret covered the fasteners with her hands and shook her head. "I want to do this." Her lips explored his bare midsection as she freed another clasp.

Ayden groaned. "You're doing that slow on purpose." He closed his eyes at the sensation of her breath on his belly, "Aren't you?"

***

Margaret James

—

Margaret suppressed a chuckle at his breathless accusation. "Are you in a rush, then?" She pressed the bulge beneath his trousers with one hand and slipped another clasp free with her other. "Perhaps I should get dressed." She cast a glance up at her dearest love.

The rise and fall of his chest showed Ayden's struggle to remain still. He balled his hands into fists at his side, and his head tipped back. "Margaret," he warned with a groan.

She swallowed a laugh. "Mind your breeze. It's getting gusty in here."

As familiar with the other's body as they could be with clothes on, they'd spent hours lying on the bed, pressed together, teasing each other as they kissed.

This exploration was long overdue.

With the next clasp, his manhood came free. Thick and veined, it bobbed slowly before Margaret's face.

"And who's this? I believe introductions are in order."

"Margaret."

"My brothers name their...theirs."

"How do you know? They wouldn't talk to you about something like that, and they only talk to each other in their heads."

"Nevertheless." She kissed the side of his penis. "It's good to meet you, oh, nameless one."

"In for a penny, eh, Margaret?" Ayden stood and removed his trousers, pausing for a moment in the dim light for her to stare. "Are you in for a pound as well?" He crawled onto the bed and tucked her to his side. They embraced in their usual positions—her head pillowed on his shoulder, his arm around her back, her leg bent across his.

"You know I am." She snuggled beneath his chin. "I've been ready.

His long arms reached to her knees, caressing up her thigh to her hips, the across her waist to cup her breast.

"Oh, that's nice." She rolled to her back, giving him greater access to both of her breasts.

Ayden rose on one elbow and lowered his face to hers. "I love you." His gentle lips and soft caress soothed her.

This was how it should always be between them—and yet an unfulfilled desire whispered in her head—*There is more.*

The kiss slowed, and his mouth dropped to her chin, then her neck, and finally, the tip of his tongue found her nipple.

"There's more," she voiced her thought, lost in the pleasure his tongue on her nipple created down deep in her belly.

"Be patient." His mouth moved to her other breast as his fingers played with the curls between her legs. "Prop your knee up, yes, like that." Then his fingertips ran up and down her core, teasing her and leaving her breathless.

"I never imagined...." Her words ended in a small gasp as he found her sensitive nub. The burst of sensation shocked her, and she grabbed his wrist.

His gaze rose to hers as his knuckle continued to circle, just out of reach of the tiny heart. "Too much?"

"Maybe," she sighed. "It surprised me." Her head fell back onto the mattress. "I've never felt anything like this." Her hips rose in time with the rhythm of his touch. Margaret closed her eyes to let the wonder of this new magic wash over her. Her senses came alive. The air circulating in the overheated room touched her, another aspect of Ayden that caressed her entire body. His hand sought the most intimate parts of her and brought a reaction she never imagined.

He changed the circular rhythm of his hand and slid a finger inside her. Round and round became in and out. All the while, he continued to excite the sensitive nub of flesh with one motion.

Her hips rose to meet each thrust of his hand. Then two fingers fluttered inside her, another sensation she never dreamed possible. "What are you doing?" Her gaze met his in the semi-darkness.

"Do you like that? I'm trying to make sure I don't hurt you too much."

"Hurt me?"

He looked down at her hand between her legs and nodded. "Two fingers barely fit. Are you sure this doesn't hurt?"

"Not at all—but don't stop the other part. Yes, that. I like that."

He chuckled softly. "Give me your hand." He wrapped her palm around his shaft. As her fingers tightened, he took a shuddering breath, "I like your touch too."

Margaret marveled at the hardness in her hand. It could have been stone-covered in satin.

Ayden groaned at her soft exploration. "I don't think I can wait any longer."

"Wait?"

He spread her legs wider and knelt between them. "I don't want to hurt you."

"I don't think you will."

"I might, and I couldn't bear it if I do. There might be a better way." He collapsed beside her and grinned at her confusion. "On your knees, my lady, I'm putting you in charge."

"Me?" She moved to the side, giving him the middle of the small bed.

"One leg over. Now move up." He pulled her thighs forward until they straddled his hips. His hands slid up her thighs to her backside. He kneaded her buttocks firmly, pulling to either side, opening her vagina, then running his fingertips down her center to the sensitive nubbin, then back up.

A warmth curled between her legs, growing hotter each time the tips of his fingers descended and tighter as they moved away from her sensitive essence.

Her senses drew inward, and she rocked against his hands, demanding more of—something.

She gasped as the taut sensation between her legs released, expanding upward into her lower belly. The pulsating relief came again and then again.

She jerked when Ayden touched the nub. "Don't—it's too sensitive now." Another pulse of pleasure tightened and released between her legs. "Dear Goddess, that was—I've never felt anything like it."

"Rub yourself on me, yes, like that." Ayden closed his eyes as she moved her wet opening up and down his manhood. His hand slid between them and lifted his shaft. "Now, take me inside."

Margaret eased down, the tip pressing into her.

"Lift up and then down again, just a bit further." His eyes remained closed. His jaw clenched and tight.

"I think this hurts you more than me," Margaret observed. She lifted and lowered, sliding his shaft further inside each time.

"It doesn't hurt...it feels wonderful. I'm trying not to let it end too soon." His palm cupped her breast and rubbed her nipple with his thumb. The other hand remained between them, raised at an angle that let her brush her most sensitive spot against him each time she descended.

"How does this end?" She rose and lowered again. The pleasurable stretch inside her warred with the burn in her thighs.

"Getting tired?"

"My legs—"

"Let's switch." Ayden wrapped his arm around her hips, lifted them both with the other arm, then rolled her beneath him in a single motion.

"Ah!" The move drove him completely inside Margaret. The sharp strike of pain surprised her but faded just as fast.

Ayden withdrew and plunged, holding her hips steady. His mouth found hers as the passion between them mounted.

She ran her palms down his slick, sweat-soaked back, then plied her nails softly along his spine as he moved within her.

His motion became shorter and faster, the arm around her hips lifted to press her mound tight to his. He rose on one elbow and stared into her face with half-closed eyes. "I love you, Margaret," he whispered.

"I love you too, Ayden. I'll love you forever."

He swelled inside, and his rocking motion stopped. Eyes closed, he shuddered as his pleasure found him. Ayden pressed into her again. His arms trembled, and he lowered himself to lie half atop her with his face buried in the hair beside her neck. After a few deep breaths, he withdrew from her and rolled to her side, tucking her back into their usual position, her head on his shoulder, her knee angled across his thigh.

After Ayden fell into a light sleep, Margaret eased from the bed to clean herself. A damp cloth wiped between her legs showed a tiny bit of blood mixed with semen and her fluids.

I must bring extra towels and water to the apartment.

She fully intended to explore this new side of their relationship, now that they were bound by deed as man and wife, if not by words.

Ayden's oversized white shirt had dried in his magical breeze, and she pulled it over her nakedness then worked the bottom button to keep the material closed around her legs. She stared at the closed window curtain and recalled the strong response her body had to Ayden's touch, the sense of him moving inside her. So focused on her recollection, she jumped at his soft touch on her arms.

Ayden moved back and lifted his hands. "I didn't mean to startle you."

"I was thinking about our evening." She looked at the small bed and shoved several strands of hair from her face. "And how I will need to plan for this type of encounter from now on." She raised an eyebrow and grinned.

"If we get caught, fully clothed and sitting at the table, it would be bad. But if someone were to walk in while we are in the middle of—" Ayden gestured at the rumpled bedding. "Margaret, it would ruin your reputation, and your mother would have me arrested."

She fought the urge to laugh at his concerns. Instead, she leaned over the table and allowed his shirt to gap open from her shoulder to her thighs. "Don't worry so much. Everything will be all right." She flicked the single button out of its hole and stepped into his arms. "I love you so much."

Ayden blinked several times, then shook his head slightly. "And I love you." He kissed her lightly then lifted his head. "But we can't overlook how dangerous it is for us to meet like this, and now—"

"Shh." She placed a finger on his lips. "Then let's run away."

"Yes. But I'll need to save enough for train fare and to pay rent and feed us until I can secure employment."

"How long? Next week? Next month?"

Ayden shook his head. "It will be closer to next year. I'll put aside money each week, but I also support my family." He hesitated, lost in thought, then turned his gaze back to her. "Once my father finds permanent employment, their needs will lessen, and we can make firmer plans. Until then, we must take extra precautions not to get caught."

She wrapped her arms around his body, pressing her naked chest to his. "I will wait forever to be with you." She tipped her head to gaze into his eyes.

"I won't make you wait that long." His lips found hers as his arms crushed her to his side.

When the kiss broke, she slipped out of his shirt and handed it to him. "I need to return before the cook begins her baking."

His eyes traveled the length of her nakedness as he slipped on his shirt. "If I did not tell you enough how stunning you are, let me say one last time. You astound me with your beauty."

His devouring gaze embarrassed her, but she raised her chin, then tipped her head at the compliment. "Next week then? Same time?"

"Yes." He finished dressing. "I will think of nothing but you until then."

Margaret pulled her skirt over her hips and attached the clasp. "Be careful on your way home."

He kissed her quickly, cradling her face in his work-roughened hands. "And you as well." Then he slipped out the door and was gone.

Margaret pulled on her camisole then straightened the carriage apartment. She waited to the count of one hundred, then doused the light with a thought and slipped into the early morning darkness.

Chapter 14

Bernard James

—

December 1848 - Beacon Hill

Bernard crossed the snowy yard from the carriage house to the kitchen mudroom, his brother a half-step behind him.

They had passed the last decent inn four hours ago, determined to make it to Boston tonight from their tour of the southern sweep of properties. They collected December's rent and gifted the tenants January's as a Christmas present from the James Family. Even though they didn't celebrate the holiday like their Christian occupants, they both enjoyed the surprise and appreciation shown by the tenants.

Last year we gave them a ham, Bay whispered into his mind.

They appeared to like this much better, Bernard replied

Bernard shook the snow from his hat and hung his hat, coat, and wool scarf on pegs beside the door.

We should have stopped at the inn, though. Bayard thought to him as he sat to remove his boots.

And tomorrow, you would have wished we'd rode on. Bernard's boots landed beside his brother's.

They separated at the top of the stairs—Bayard to his room at the front of the house. Bernard to his, a comfortable room down the hall from their sister, overlooking the backyard and carriage house.

Ignoring the lamp, he unknotted the silk tie from his neck, tossed it at the wardrobe, and slipped his jacket off.

Do not wake me in the morning, Bayard warned

You'll be up before I am. You always are. Bernard pulled the link from his cuff when movement on the ground below caught his attention. As he worked the other cufflink, he leaned closer to the glass and watched a cloaked figure slip through the back gate and hurry across the yard to the kitchen door.

We have a maid creeping in from a lover's tryst, he relayed to Bay.

Do you know how little I care? I'm trying to sleep.

Bernard dropped both cufflinks into his jewelry case and unbuttoned his shirt.

Outside his door, soft footsteps swept past, and then the door to Margaret's room shut with care.

It was Margaret!

Bernard pressed his ear to their adjoining wall but heard nothing from the room next door.

Did you hear me? Our sister is running about in the middle of the night.

Unlikely.

I know what I saw, and I heard her enter her room.

Go to bed, Bern. You can ask Margaret about it in the morning.

"And she'll deny it," Bernard mumbled to himself as he slid beneath the covers. Just what in the Lord and Lady's name was going on?

He slept poorly and left his bed to dress just after sunrise.

Downstairs, he found his mother in her dressing gown having her morning tea and biscuit.

"I didn't know you were back. What time did you get in?" She placed her porcelain cup on its saucer and gave him her full attention.

"Before the kitchen was awake." He took the seat across from her. "And before Margaret came in."

"Margaret? What are you talking about?"

He glanced around the room, looking toward the staircase, then the kitchen opening, before he lowered his voice and leaned forward. "I saw my little sister sneak into the house after Bay and I returned. I heard her go into her room."

Chantal folded her hands in her lap and stared at her son. "That is a most peculiar and alarming accusation."

"I saw her with my own eyes. There is no doubt."

"I'd suspect she was meeting Robert, but he isn't due home for another few months."

"Who?"

"A suitor. Never mind. It doesn't matter." Chantal tapped her finger on the table and chewed thoughtfully on the side of her cheek.

"You need to speak with her," Bernard insisted. "She can't be allowed to galivant around at all hours to who knows where."

"And if I tell her to stop, and she doesn't, what then? Set a guard? Ship her off?" Chantal shook her head. "Until we know what she's doing and who she meets, it will do us no good."

"Then what do you suggest?"

"Follow her, but don't let her know you're there. Discover who she meets and where, then we'll know how to end this for good."

Bernard sat back and stared hard at his mother. "Why me?"

"Why not you? Your room is next to hers. You're the one who has discovered her nighttime escapades." She picked up her tea and sipped.

"I thought you'd be more concerned."

Who should be concerned? Bayard asked.

Go back to sleep, Bay.

"I am deeply concerned. But once we have all the related information, I'm sure we will easily handle the rest of this tawdry business." Chantal poured another cup of tea. "We can't have her nocturnal antics made public."

Bernard nodded. His mother understood the consequences of the situation.

"Now, let me finish my tea. Get back to me when you have more information." She sipped then looked up as he stood. "Oh, and keep this from your brother if you can. He has a soft spot for your sister."

"That will be difficult."

"But good practice. No one should know all your secrets, my boy. Not even your twin."

One week later, near midnight, quiet movements in the hallway outside his door alerted Bernard. He dressed in the dark as he watched Margaret cross the small lawn to the back gate and slip into the alleyway.

Her footprints in the fresh snow led out the gate. They didn't go far—just past the carriage house next door.

Bernard crossed the narrow back street and waited beside a similar building that lined the alleyway.

Less than twenty minutes later, a man rounded the corner and tossed something over the fence at the end of the lane. Then the fellow hurried to their neighbor's gate and entered. The same gate where Margaret's footsteps ended.

Smoke soon rose from the carriage house chimney next door.

Bernard rubbed his hands together, then pulled on an old pair of mittens he'd stuffed into his pockets.

It was surprisingly bright outside. The low-hanging clouds reflected the lights of the city and harbor. He moved closer to the neighbor's gate and found a convenient shadow to stand in.

He didn't have long to wait.

***

Ayden MacKenna

—

Ayden pulled the heavy quilted cover over their bodies and tucked her next to his heart. "You're anxious tonight," he observed, still trying to catch his breath.

"I know." Margaret nodded, shoving the hair from her eyes. "My brothers are back. They'll be home for at least a month." She looked up at him with all the love and trust in her heart. "I think Bay would understand—about us—but Bern and mother..." she shuddered.

"We'll need to be cautious." He kissed her forehead. "Perhaps we should not meet here until after they leave again."

"I'd hate that." She hugged him and sniffed.

"Me too."

"The next full moon is on the eighth, after the new year. They'll be out of the house that night. They try never to miss a coven meeting."

Ayden kissed her nose as he left the bed and pulled on his trousers. "The night of the eighth then." He pulled on his boots then shrugged into his shirt. "Three weeks."

Margaret nodded and held the covering up to her chin as she sat up. "I wish we didn't have to sneak about like this."

Ayden glanced at the coal stove, and the flames snuffed out. "It won't be long until the sneaking is done. I've saved enough for train tickets and more besides. A few months, and we'll be off to New York."

"A few? Two? Six?" She swung her legs from under the cover, reached for her skirt, then stood as she lifted the material.

Ayden eyed her breasts until she pulled her camisole over her head and down to her waist.

Margaret tucked the longer edges beneath the waistband of her skirt.

"Closer to two, maybe three, to be safe. I want to leave my family a bit to get by on until I can send more from New York."

"Your mother's no better?"

Ayden pushed his arms into his coat and worked a few buttons. "She is, and then she isn't. She's changed since Mel was born. I don't think she'll ever be the same."

"That's so sad. I'm sorry." Margaret crossed the small space, wrapped her arms around him, and rose on her toes to kiss him. "We'll send them all we can once we are away from here."

Ayden kissed her back, then wrapped an old woolen scarf around his neck and ears. He finished his outerwear with the top hat Mr. Murphy had given him for Christmas last year. "Get home safe, sweetheart. I'll see you on the eighth."

Margaret blew him a kiss as he closed the door.

The wind caught at the edge of his jacket and finished buttoning his overcoat. He quickly rounded the corner of the carriage house and into the alley, closing the latch softly. He paused to look up at the cloud cover, aglow with reflected light from the city. It looked like more snow.

He hoped Sampson had found a warm bed inside tonight. Then he hurried down the alley toward home.

$$***$$

Bernard James

—

I have him!

For a moment, Bernard thought he might not be able to identify the libertine, but the cad turned toward him and lifted his face to the sky.

Ayden MacKenna. I should have guessed.

Bernard quickly shuttered his thoughts not to wake his brother.

Had it not been for his immense respect for the strength of that bastard's fire-skill, he would have burned him to ash where he stood. Instead, he waited until MacKenna rounded the corner, then Bernard bolted for home. He wanted to be in his room before his sister returned to the house.

He hid his wet boots behind his brother's boots in the mudroom and hurried upstairs. He watched Margaret enter through the carriage house gate and cross the small yard from his darkened window.

What are you doing up? Bayard's thought came to him

Bernard winced.

Keeping his thoughts shuttered from his twin was not something he consciously did.

The maid snuck out again tonight. Not a complete fabrication.

Back to the maid, are we? Go to bed, Bernard.

Yes. Sorry to have woken you.

Margaret's soft step in the hall and careful close of her door angered Bernard all over again. He sat on the edge of his bed and ran a hand through his hair, wondering what could be done to avert a tragedy of Margaret's own making.

Another restless night found Bernard awake at dawn. He closed his thoughts and hurried down to breakfast to speak with his mother.

She dipped a bit of sweet roll into her tea and glanced up as he entered the dining room. "You've discovered something, I can tell."

"Good morning, Mother—and yes. I know who she meets." He settled into the chair across from her and waved off the cook. Once the cook returned to the kitchen, he leaned forward. "Ayden MacKenna."

His mother choked on her roll, set the piece on the dish, and raised her napkin to her lips. A moment later, her gaze rose to meet his. "Are you certain?"

"I am. Margaret and MacKenna met last night in the carriage house next door. I followed her and waited until I saw him. I saw his face. There is no doubt it was MacKenna."

Composure reclaimed; Chantal folded the napkin and set it beside her plate. "We must handle this delicately."

"Why not call him out? He's ruined our sister!" Bernard exclaimed in a harsh whisper.

"Think, Bernard. If the affair is made public, they will be forced to marry." Chantal shook her head. "We can't have that. No one must know."

"What do you propose then?" He shuttered his mind so tightly his head ached.

"Stay quiet for now. Go about your business as usual." Her voice dropped to a whisper. "Find out where he works, where he lives, where he goes, and who his friends are. Be alert for an opportunity to rid ourselves of this scoundrel. But your sister must not know, nor your brother until the last moment."

"I understand." He picked up a roll from the tray, then rang the handbell on the table. "Tea," he said to the cook as she looked in.

"What will you do?" he asked his mother as she rose from the table.

"I think Margaret and I will call on Mrs. Prescott today to see how she's feeling."

"Who is this?"

"Never mind, dear. Just do as I asked," Chantal's voice dwindled as she left the room. "Good morning, Bay. You should join Bernard for breakfast. There are sweet rolls."

Chapter 15

Chantal James

—

February 1849 - Beacon Hill

Chantal removed her leather gloves, pulling one finger loose at a time, and handed them to the maid in her entry. Her winter bonnet followed the gloves and then the long jacket. "Tell the cook to bring tea to the morning room."

"Yes, ma'am."

Chantal smoothed her hair as she crossed to the east-facing room. She took a seat on the settee facing the window to consider what she'd learned.

Mrs. Prescott, Robert's mother, had taken a turn. She'd been too weak to come down for a visit Chantal scheduled to discuss their children's future.

Chantal happened to meet Agatha's physician in the Prescott entry as he prepared to leave. He confided that telegrams would be sent to several pre-arranged ports today to ask both her husband and her son to return home without delay. The doctor did not know when or where the message might reach the two men, but he did not expect Mrs. Prescott to see her spring flowers bloom.

So Robert will be coming home.

It was about time.

Chantal and Bernard had allowed Margaret to sneak from the house repeatedly without saying a word. But it had not been easy to keep Bernard silent and ignore her daughter's shameless behavior.

Her tea arrived and she relaxed back and took a sip of the warm brew.

Chantal intended to use Agatha's declining health as a reason Robert and Margaret should marry immediately. Robert's poor mother deserved the chance to see her only son wed, after all. Once married, Margaret's scandalous affair would be her husband's problem, not her mother's.

Chantal's frayed nerves had begun to settle when Bernard stomped through the front door scattering snow across the entry.

He handed his hat and coat to the maid, then caught Chantal's stare. He made straight for the sitting room. "I've news."

"Let's hope it's interesting. Take your boots off." Chantal rang the bell on the table. "Another cup and saucer for my son." She held up a finger to her son to hold his information. "I've news as well, and I shall go first."

"As you wish." Bootless, Bernard settled into the chair across from the settee.

"Agatha Prescott is on her deathbed. The doctor believes she only has a few weeks to live."

"I'm sorry, mother. Who is dying?"

The maid brought in another saucer and teacup. "Would you like me to pour?"

"No. That will be all." Chantal dismissed the young woman, then narrowed her eyes at her son. "Robert's mother. Your sister's suitor? The doctor has sent for her son to return home from the sea."

"And you think that will solve our...problem? I'm not sure I agree with your assessment." Bernard poured a cup from the porcelain teapot and leaned back in his chair. "You underestimate her stubbornness."

"It will at least make it more difficult for –ugh." Chantal took a sip of tea. "It is simply too vulgar to contemplate."

"I may have discovered a solution." Bernard smiled and raised the teacup to his lips.

"And?"

"Bayard and I had lunch with an interesting foreign fellow at a restaurant near the harbor. He's a shipowner, just made port from India."

"I'm not sure I see the point—"

"He approached us, drew us aside, and declared he could see we were witches because he can read auras. Our auras gave us away as *skilled*."

"Go on."

"He is in the market for a magic-using servant to return with him to India. I got the impression there was a great deal he didn't divulge. However, after an extended discussion over lunch, I learned he would not be opposed to an indentured individual. Willing or not, should the opportunity for the right person present itself."

Chantal swallowed. Her teacup rattled as she set it on the table. "India, you say. How long does he plan to be in port?"

"As long as it takes to secure a servant of the right caliber—magically speaking, one able to manipulate fire."

"And he could *see* you and Bayard are skilled with *Fire*."

Bernard nodded. "I believe you should speak with him."

"I believe you are right. Can you arrange a meeting?"

"I already have. If you are agreeable, this man can meet with you on his ship tomorrow morning at ten. Bayard and I will accompany you for your visit."

"Good. Excellent. Where is your brother?"

"Showing our new friend around Boston. I didn't think you'd want us to bring the fellow here."

"Quite right. What does Bayard think?"

"Bay thinks an apprenticeship in India would be an exciting opportunity for a young witch who might wish to broaden their horizons. He mentioned several of the new coven members as possible candidates."

"Then he has no suspicions?"

"None."

"And what is our new friend's name?

"Aamir Rakesh Kapoor."

Dressed in her warmest day dress, fur muff, and bonnet, Chantal stepped from the James coach and walked to the gangway of the foreign ship. Holding Bernard's arm, she mounted the ramp and boarded the sleek three-mast vessel.

A dark-skinned man in loose-fitting attire bowed to her as she paused on the deck. "Magi Rakesh awaits you in the captain's cabin." Shorter than Chantal, he extended his arm. "This way, please." He pointed to ropes and lines. "Mind your step, please."

Chantal exchanged a look with her son and stepped carefully around the equipment.

The servant opened the door beside the stair that led to the quarterdeck and stepped back. "Please enter."

Glass windows lined the cabin walls, filling the room with winter light. Seated behind a polished oak desk, Magi Rakesh stood and bowed. "Welcome. I am Aamir Rakesh Kapoor. You may address me as Magi Rakesh." He indicated two chairs on the other side of the desk. "Please, to be seated."

"Thank you, no." With no servant to take her outerwear, Chantal did not intend to stay long. "I prefer to come to an understanding quickly and take our leave."

"As you wish." Dark-skinned and handsome, with a neatly trimmed beard and mustache, Rakesh wore a turban above his American-style suit. He rounded the side of the desk and rested his hip against the edge. "Your sons have told you I seek an apprentice—one skilled in the ways of *fire magic?*"

"They have, and we have a candidate in mind."

"As strong as you and your sons? I can see you all share an inclination for *Fire.*" He spoke English with only a slight accent. His teeth were white and straight beneath his dark mustache."

"The young man we would put forth is a strong *Fire-Elementalist.*"

"A requirement, as I stated to your sons." Rakesh stood away from the desk and crossed his arms. "How old is this man?"

"A year or so younger than my twins. The perfect age to become an apprentice. There is, however, one slight problem. He will not accept your apprenticeship willingly."

Rakesh stroked his beard, narrowed his eyes, and studied Chantal. "That is not a problem for me, should I decide to bestow this student with all I know. But I wonder," he shifted his gaze to Bernard, "why I should accept an unwilling person when my offer is most attractive. Certainly, I could find a willing candidate. I am most perplexed."

"The individual we propose is proven adept at pyromancy. In fact, he foresaw my husband's death but failed to act upon this knowledge until it was too late."

"I begin to understand." Rakesh paced to the side window that overlooked the harbor. "How long ago did this incident take place?"

"Almost seven and a half years ago."

"A cold dish then." Rakesh put his back to the window and crossed his arms. "If I agree to take this man against his will, how much do you wish to be paid?"

"No payment will be required or accepted." Perspiration tickled the back of Chantal's neck. "I only need your guarantee he will not return to this city for, let's say, at least six months."

"A fire magus skilled in pyromancy at no cost? I must accept your proposal." He bowed to Chantal. "When might I expect you to bring me this young man?"

"Within the week." She motioned for Bernard to open the door. "I will send you a missive before delivery."

"I will require your presence."

Chantal halted in the doorway. "Whatever for?"

"It is my one requirement. You must witness the bonding of the one you intend to send into servitude."

"Must I?" Chantal considered, then gave a sharp nod of agreement at Rakesh. She left the cabin and crossed the deck to the gangway.

The turbaned servant bowed as they left the ship.

"What do we tell Bay?" Bernard followed down the ramp to the dock.

"Tell him nothing until we capture MacKenna."

"Taking MacKenna won't be easy."

Chantal turned, enraged at her son and the indignity of dealing with a foreigner who offered no refreshment and had no servant take her coat. "Must I do all your thinking for you?"

Bernard remained stone-faced. "Not at all, mother."

"Fine then." She spun back toward the carriage and continued. "Advise me when you have a date."

Chapter 16

Ayden MacKenna

—

Ayden tapped the point of the pencil several times on the ledger, then completed the entry. Lost in thoughts of last night with Margaret, he raised his head and gazed out of the room's small window. Tonight would be his last night with his parents and Melvyn. Tomorrow's sunrise would see Margaret and him on the train to New York.

Early morning snow clung to the rooftops and cobblestone streets. Overhead, a clear blue sky belied the chilly temperature outdoors. A whisper of spring had come to New England, but softly.

The bell above the door downstairs rang as a customer entered the store.

Since his promotion to assistant manager, Ayden no longer worried about orders or deliveries on the sales floor; instead, he met with wholesale merchants, sometimes at their ships in the harbor and sometimes at their mills outside of Boston. He kept the balance sheets for the mercantile and helped Mr. Murphy train and hire store employees.

"Ayden, you still up there?" Murphy's voice carried up the stockroom stairs.

Ayden closed the ledger and slipped it into the desk drawer. "I am, sir," he called as he came to his feet. "I'll be right down."

A young messenger waited at the back of the mercantile. "Mr. MacKenna?"

Ayden nodded. "Yes. Is this for me?"

"Yes, sir." The lad bobbed his head and handed Ayden the missive. "From a big ship in port—a Captain Leonid."

Ayden traded a penny for the message, and the youngster tugged his cap and skipped out of the store.

"An unexpected shipment?" Mr. Murphy asked.

"Yes." Ayden slipped the message into his pocket. "It could be the first ship from Cuba with sugar, molasses, and tobacco. It'll be more expensive due to the tariffs, but it would be the first one in port this year. I don't know this captain though."

"Take a look at what he has to offer. You know what we can charge and still make a profit."

Ayden grabbed his long coat and hat from the coat rack in the stock room. "I'll be back as soon as I can."

"Take your time."

The chill breeze tried to unseat his top hat, which he promptly tapped down firmly on his head. The short walk to the docks, at first anticipated due to the sunshine, turned miserable as the wind clutched at his neck, reminding him he'd forgotten his scarf.

In the brisk, damp weather, few people ventured onto the street. Ayden cut through the alleyway behind the waterfront shops. Above the roofline, wooden masts stood tall against the deceptive blue sky.

Near the corner ahead, a pedestrian braved the weather. Collar turned up, his back to the passage, the man loitered casually facing the waterfront—the size and shape of the individual vaguely familiar.

Ayden recognized the man as he turned. The alarmed expression on Bayard's face made his heart skip a beat.

Has something happened to Margaret?

Before he could call out, a blow to the back of his head sent him to his knees. Ayden gasped with pain as his vision swam in and out of focus.

Bayard rushed toward Ayden, but a second blow from behind drove the blue sky from his sight.

***

Bayard James

—

"What the hell, Bern? You've killed him!" Bayard rolled the unconscious young man onto his back and felt for a pulse.

"He's not dead, at least not yet." Bernard tossed the metal bar down into the muddy passage. He gathered Ayden's legs, one beneath each arm. "Well, come on then, mum's waiting on the ship."

"Was this the plan all along?" Bayard lifted his coven member's weight with a grunt, bumping the unconscious man's head against his shoulder. "Whatever this is, it's wrong, and you know it."

Ayden's hat had fallen to the ground with the blow to his head and then crushed beneath Bernard's booted feet. "Lord and Lady, he's heavy."

The ship where their mother waited was just beyond the waterfront road. A bitter gust assaulted the men as they carried their charge up the boarding ramp.

A sailor opened a hatch on the deck and waved the brothers forward. The swarthy-skinned man nodded and pointed toward the darkness below.

"Down here!" Chantal called out, and her face appeared, reflecting the brilliant light of day.

"Can you make it?" Bernard asked.

Bayard grunted and adjusted the weight in his arms. "He's heavy. I don't know if I can manage stairs."

A brief conversation took place between the sailor on deck and an unseen individual below. The sailor nodded, then reached down and pulled the wooden ladder from the hold.

"Toss him down," a heavily accented male voice instructed.

"Toss him?" Bayard exclaimed. "That will surely kill him."

Bernard released Ayden's legs and kicked the unconscious man's boots until they dangled into the opening.

"There is hay down here. It will break the fall," Chantal called from the dark hold.

Bayard walked his burden forward, crouching as Ayden's lower body disappeared into the hole in the deck. "Bern, grab his arm. We can lower him a bit more."

Bernard heaved a sigh. "Why do you care, Bay. It's not like he's a friend."

Bayard glared until his brother gripped Ayden's arm, and they lowered the man into the hold.

"That's good. Let go now," the foreign voice instructed.

The brothers released Ayden, and a dull thump sounded from below.

"Get to the carriage." Chantal's face reappeared. "I'll only be a moment longer, and we shall be on our way."

"This is wrong," Bayard muttered as they marched down the ramp to the dock.

"No one will know. Besides, think of the exotic apprenticeship in India. If Ayden doesn't like it, he can come back whenever he likes," Bernard argued.

"No. There is no honor in this." Bayard glanced back at the ship bobbing in the harbor. "None whatsoever."

***

Chantal James

———

"There is your *fire-witch*. I believe the terms of our agreement are now complete."

"Almost." The turbaned man lifted a thin stack of paper. "An unwilling indentured apprentice must sign a contract," he looked from Ayden to Chantal, "in blood."

Chantal narrowed her eyes at Rakesh. "Let me see that." She jerked the papers from the man's hand and quickly scanned the words. "At least this is in English."

"A requirement. The binding will only work if written in the apprentice's native language."

"I see." She flipped the page. "This says twenty years from today." Chantal grinned. "I doubt you'll be able to keep him that long, but you're welcome to try."

"He is so strong then?"

"His magic is extraordinarily strong. A prodigy, or so I've heard it whispered."

"And a pyromancer as well?"

"For all the good it's done him, yes." She handed the contract back. "So now what?"

"It must be his blood and the mark made by his hand. I cannot assist."

"Very well. Hold your papers close." Chantal lifted Ayden's hand by the wrist, bending the elbow and rubbing the fingers into the sticky wet mass at the back of her victim's head. Her lips drew back in disgust as she guided Ayden's hand, fingers red with blood, and placed a mark on the bottom of the paperwork. "Is that good enough?" She dropped Ayden's arm and checked her gloves for blood, then swept her skirt away from the unconscious man at her feet.

"It will suffice." Rakesh chuckled and folded the papers into his pocket. He called toward the light above, and the sailor's face appeared briefly, then the ladder reappeared. Rakesh steadied the stairs until they were secured above. He bowed from the waist to Chantal. "It has been my pleasure, madam. You will understand if I do not escort you from the ship. I must see to my passenger's comfort for our voyage. We set sail immediately."

"Yes, that is best." Misgivings flooded Chantal's mind, but there was no other way. This meager merchant would not sully her daughter's reputation. Instead, Margaret would wed within the ranks of the Brahmin, as Chantal had planned. Her daughter would never need to worry about the prophecy that had haunted Chantal for most of her life.

Out of the dank and dark hold, she spotted her sons and their family carriage near the ship's ramp.

The dark-skinned sailor escorted Chantal from the vessel.

As she arranged her skirt in the carriage, she glanced through the window and noticed the ramp already stowed and the vessel unmoored. Rakesh and his ship would sail at high tide.

Taking the troublesome Ayden MacKenna with them.

***

Margaret James

—

Bags packed and stowed beneath her bed; Margaret waited impatiently for the house to quiet for the night. Beneath the covers, she wore her traveling dress and stockings. Her shoes, cloak, and two clean dresses were folded neatly in a large old pillowcase.

She didn't dare try to carry her large travel trunk down the stairs. She would retrieve her shoes and cloak once she escaped the house. Ayden would be waiting for her, she knew, with the tickets he purchased for their train ride to New York. In their new town, Ayden would find work, and they would live happily ever after.

It was just past midnight when she eased her heels into her sturdiest pair of shoes and hurried out the back gate, careful not to allow the latch to drop and rattle in the night.

Surprised to find the carriage apartment dark and empty, she struck a match and sent the flame to the oil lamps beside the bed and on the table. She dropped her filled pillowcase in the chair and took a tense seat on the bed. Ayden would be here anytime.

After an hour, she curled up on top of the covers, her eyes heavy with weariness and disappointment. She'd hear Ayden when he came in. No sense in staying awake. He would be here to take her away at any moment.

Chapter 17

Margaret James

—

March 1849 - Beacon Hill

Dressed in black, Margaret sat beside Robert on the concrete bench in her backyard garden. Snow littered the dead and broken flowers from last fall, but the sun warmed her skin and dark clothes—the sky above, blue, and free from clouds.

"Thank you for sitting with me. I had to get out of the house." Dressed for his mother's funeral, Robert tugged at his collar. His suntanned skin seemed out of place alongside the pale and silent mourners gathered in his home.

"I understand. I know your mother had been sick for quite some time, but it's still a shock when you lose someone you love."

Robert nodded. "My father is furious over her death and at me."

"At you? Whatever for?"

"He doesn't want to leave the house empty when we return to the sea." Robert glanced at Margaret, then looked away. "He threatened to disinherit me and sell the house should I not marry and install a wife immediately."

"What? That is cruel."

"He says I should have married already and that my wife would have helped care for my mother, and then she might not have died."

"The nurse and the doctor were with her almost constantly this last month. I'm not sure there would have been more your wife could have done."

"Nevertheless, marry, I must."

Margaret shook her head in disbelief. "I don't know what to say."

Robert nodded, rubbing his palms together. "And what of you? When last we spoke, there was an unacceptable suitor who had captured your interest."

Margaret's chin quivered. She swallowed and looked away, quickly wiping a tear from her eyes. Finally, unable to find her voice, she shook her head and covered her face with her gloved hands.

"Oh my dear, I'm so sorry." Robert wrapped his arms around her and rubbed her back as she cried. "I wouldn't have brought it up if I'd thought things had gone wrong. There now, it will be all right."

Margaret hadn't allowed herself to cry since Ayden disappeared, and there was no one she could speak with who would understand her despair.

She had searched for him, unable to believe he would abandon her and their plans to run away and build a life together.

At Ayden's work, Mr. Murphy acknowledged Ayden never returned after being called to the docks that morning. Later that same day, Murphy spoke with the harbor police. They found Ayden's top hat crushed near the pier, and Murphy identified it as the one he'd given his employee for Christmas. But nothing else had been discovered.

Murphy asked Margaret to take Ayden's final wages to his parents. Perhaps they would know where their son had gone. He gave her his parents' address and an envelope of cash.

But Ayden's parents did not know their child's fate either. They took the cash she offered from Murphy but did not invite Margaret inside. Ayden's parents were not as she remembered them, worn thin with worry and loss. Life on the North End had not been easy for the MacKenna family.

Margaret caught a glimpse of a small dark-haired lad clinging to his mother's skirt as Mr. MacKenna closed the door.

That had been three weeks ago.

Robert offered her his handkerchief, and Margaret wiped her face.

The torrent of emotion had engulfed her and then disappeared. "I'm sorry for that. I don't know what came over me."

"It's quite all right. Today's a day for tears. No one will think worse of you for them."

Margaret nodded. "So, what do you intend to do?"

"About my father's decree?"

"Yes." She caught an errant tear with the folded cloth.

"Get married, I suppose." Robert shrugged. "I have no idea to whom."

"Really?"

He turned his head toward her and narrowed his eyes. "There's that tone."

"Oh, Robert. There's only one person who would marry you on short notice to save your inheritance."

"You? Are you saying you would be willing to marry me?" He lifted his top hat and ran the other hand through his thick dark hair, his face filled with conflict. "I'm not sure I could do that to you."

"To me? Robert, you would be giving me a home, a life, and the freedom of a Brahmin wife."

They both chuckled, but Robert grew serious once more. "It would mean months of loneliness for you while I voyage."

"You won't sail forever. And you'll have someone who waits for your return." She took his hand. "But there are things you don't know about me, things that might make a difference—"

"No." He took her hand in both of his. "We both know there are things we have never discussed. Things we may learn of as our life together matures, but nothing that will ever come between us, our friendship, or our life together."

"I'm not sure about that," Margaret whispered.

"I'm sure." Robert dropped to one knee in the snow on the path. "Margaret, will you do me the honor of becoming my wife?"

"You know I will." She leaned forward and pressed her lips to his—a kiss to seal the bargain between them. She felt a pang of disappointment that the kiss didn't turn into more.

Give it time.

"Your mother is watching us from the window." Robert stood and dusted his knee.

 "Does she look happy?"

"I can never tell with your mother."

Margaret looked over her shoulder, and her gaze met her mother's.

Chantal smiled coolly and gave her daughter a nod, then backed from the window.

"Was that happy?" Robert inquired.

"Like the cat that ate the canary, I suppose."

"You don't think she'd object to an expedient wedding, do you?"

"No. I don't think my mother would mind at all." Margaret turned her back to the house. "Let's find your father and tell him, but wait to announce our plans until tomorrow, out of respect for your mother."

"Very well, Mrs. Prescott." Robert presented his arm.

Margaret took his arm and smiled. An honest smile, probably the first since she lost Ayden.

Damn you, Ayden, for leaving me here alone.

They walked past the carriage apartment, and Margaret lifted her chin. Her life would go on, thanks to Robert. Somehow, she found it in her heart to hope Ayden had found a measure of peace wherever he was now.

A Sneak Peek of Pyromancer

The Soul of the Witch Saga continues in Book 2:
Pyromancer

Chapter 1

Ayden MacKenna

—

March 1869—Rajputana, India

Ayden bowed his respect to the fiery brazier perched on the stone altar and pulled a white linen cloth over the pan of ash in his hands. He backed away from the raised dais beside the sacred pool. The clear water reflected burning torches along the far wall and the Zoroastrian altar's holy flame.

He pivoted at the door and stepped from the tiled temple floor to the dirt of a large public square. A sprinkling of sand blew across the empty stone benches surrounding the community well. The women had returned home at nightfall with the children to share supper and evening prayers with their husbands.

The vast sky stretched from lingering day to the oncoming night. The last glimmer of sunlight colored the western horizon while stars emerged, bright and close in the warm, dry air to the east. Outside the compound of clay homes and thatched roofs, the desolate sand filled the Thar Desert and stretched as far as the eye could see.

Silence held the village except for the shuffle of livestock, anxious for Ayden's evening visit. Feeding the camels and horses would be his final task before finding rest in his room at the back of the temple.

Without warning, nameless anticipation filled his chest, and Ayden hesitated. He turned on his heel, casting an anxious glance around the deserted square. A dim but steady glow along the eastern horizon outlined the hills and attracted his attention. His breath caught as the slender curve of a full moon inched above the mountains and cast its thin white light across the desert.

The spasm that passed through his chest took him by surprise. A strong current of ancient magic lifted the hair on his forearms and the nape of his neck. His limbs shuddered, and he lost all strength. The bin of ashes tumbled from his hand as he sank to his knees.

What's happening?

A gasp escaped his parched throat when the sorcerous shackles which bound him to Magi Rakesh shattered. The sudden and unexpected release from those invisible chains burned like wildfire. His fingers curled into the dirt of the village square. In the darkness, a red glow outlined his hands. The illumination lasted until the magical tie severed completely.

He'd been unconscious when the enchantment that imprisoned him stole his life. He'd awakened days later aboard a ship destined for India, compelled to serve the Magi Rakesh and forbidden to use magic to free himself. If the spell cast to bind him had been this painful, he couldn't remember it.

Since his capture, he'd traveled across the seas to India, the servant of Great Magi Rakesh. Their journey took them from Bombay to the Himalayas to the Gulf of Mannar at the tip of India. Eventually, Rakesh settled in this small Zoroastrian village east of the city of Bilara.

How long had he been enslaved? Fifteen years? Twenty?

His rare ability to read future events in fire made him valuable to the magi. At twenty-one, he'd been knocked unconscious in Boston Harbor and given to Rakesh because of his pyromancy skill. At least, that is what Rakesh believed.

Ayden thought otherwise.

He'd recognized his assailants in those desperate moments before he lost consciousness—trusted men—brothers to the young woman he loved.

A raised voice from the village's far side broke the silence, and Ayden lifted his head.

Rakesh felt the bond break as well. He'll seek to enslave me again—or kill me.

Although he'd learned much of the magi's Eastern magic, Rakesh's *elemental-animations* would be difficult, if not impossible, for Ayden to counter alone.

I've but one choice.

Escape.

Another shout from Rakesh spurred Ayden to his feet, and he raced around the temple into his small room near the animal enclosure. He snatched up a woven bag and stuffed his other set of clothes inside, along with the black robe he'd purchased from an Arab trader the year before, and pulled the pack onto his back.

Ayden picked up the amulet given to him by Gravâratav, the local priest he'd worked with since coming to this village. Rakesh had been furious with Tav for offering such a valuable gift to a servant.

He grinned at the memory, pulled the chain over his neck, tucked the red stone amulet into his kurta, and then ran from the room.

He vaulted the low stone wall of the corral with one hand and landed effortlessly amidst the animals.

Familiar with his scent, the camels and horses either nudged him for dinner or stepped aside.

Camel or horse?

A camel would afford him the greater distance, but longevity wouldn't be the problem if he couldn't outpace Rakesh.

A sprinter then, one that can climb hills.

He slipped a rope halter over the dappled gray gelding, tossed a blanket across the animal's back, and was out of time.

"Ayden-Mac!" Rakesh stood on the far side of the open square, torch in hand. "Do not attempt to flee, or you shall suffer the full weight of my wrath!"

Ayden leapt onto the gelding's back and glanced toward the magi. "You'll have to catch me, you bastard," he muttered.

Rakesh raised the torch to the night sky, threw back his head, and mumbled the incantation that would give life to one of his *elementals*.

He knows better than to use fire against me, and water would be too weak in the desert. He'll create an earth- or wind-animation.

Ayden gripped the reins as he leaned over the horse's neck and pressed soft leather boots into the animal's sides. "Yah!"

The gray took two long strides across the enclosure then cleared the corral wall with grace. They gained speed on the eastern road as the ground shook beneath them. At this pace, if the gelding tripped, the fall would kill them both.

A quarter-mile later, Ayden risked a glance over his shoulder.

An *earth-animation* followed them. The large lumbering *elemental*, raised from stone and sand, moved swifter than Ayden would have thought possible. The *animation* held the shape of a wide-chested, headless man. No fingers to grasp, its boulder-sized fists were designed to crush its prey rather than capture.

A zigzagging crack in the ground shot ahead of the monstrosity and cleaved the road, eager to catch and trip the horse.

He couldn't escape without a fight.

The only elements available for Ayden to manipulate in the empty desert were *Earth* and *Air*.

Earth was Rakesh's strongest element.

Something unexpected then.

He wrapped the leather reins around one hand, pulled the amulet from his shirt, and gripped the red stone with the other. "Caz, come forth and do my bidding."

The spark of fire within the stone flashed through Ayden's fingers and clung to the golden chain singeing his shirt. The tiny *elemental* waited near Ayden's hand for his master's command.

"Share your flame with me, Caz." Ayden opened his hand.

Fire flowed from the *elemental*, creating a blaze which Ayden rolled in his open palm. When the whirling flame filled his hand from the wrist to fingers, he hurled the tightly wound fireball at the stone golem, striking the monster in the chest.

The fireball clung to the stone and caused the beast to stumble. But it regained its footing and forged ahead. The remaining fire bled off the living rock like water.

Undeterred, Ayden threw three more orbs of fire in quick succession, but they had no more effect than the first.

The only element left to me is air.

"Caz, return."

The tiny *fire-elemental* slid into the stone, pulsating red on Ayden's chest.

In desperation, he raised his hand, pulling the dry, static heat that rose from the desert into his grip. Then he twisted his hand, casting his invocation at the *elemental* behind him.

A whirlwind lifted from the dusty road around the golem's feet as static-spawned lightning impaled the monster again and again.

The flashes blinded Ayden, and he turned away, blinking to clear his vision.

They'd come far enough from the village that the east road had made its long sweeping curve south to parallel the mountains.

British regiments often camp in these hills.

Ayden yanked the reins and directed his tiring horse into the scrub alongside the road, then up the hillside. As they crested the first low rise, he looked back.

Where Ayden's lightning found its target, large chunks of rock had split from the massive, *animated-elemental*. Thrown back at the monster by the whirling wind, the beast swatted at pieces of himself, its original objective forgotten. As Rakesh's magic failed, one of the giant's legs crumbled. The dying *animation* fell and thrashed in the road.

Dust from Ayden's windstorm filled his horse's tracks and concealed the point where they left the road.

Now to find a British camp.

It was early in the season for regiments to seek shelter from the heat in the mountains, but not impossible. If Ayden had to, he'd ride to Ajmer-Merwara and claim sanctuary as an American citizen.

He rode down a small embankment, then up a larger hill. The Aravallis were old mountains, rounded and filled with foliage as he climbed higher out of the desert. A stone cliff barred their way, and he rode south until they could ascend again.

At the top of the next rise, he drew rein and viewed the desert below.

Lights from the fires in his village remained visible to the northwest. He didn't see any *animated-elementals* on the moonlit hills behind him, but he didn't care to linger and find out.

He slid from the tired horse and walked beside the animal up the next hill. To his left, on the far side of the ridge, a campfire lit the night.

"Halt!" A command made in the Hindi language.

Ayden raised his hands.

Of course, the British army would post guards.

Why had he imagined he'd ride unchallenged into their camp?

"I'm American," he spoke English rather than Hindi. "I seek asylum."

"Asylum?" The question came from the darkness behind him in heavily accented English.

"Yes. I was held captive and only just escaped."

"Drop the reins. Are you armed?"

"I have no weapons." Ayden let the rope slip through his fingers and thought momentarily about his magic and the amulet around his neck. "I only wish to return home."

A match struck, a bright flare in the night. "And where is that?" A dark-skinned soldier in a British uniform and turban lifted a torch.

A second guard held a rifle but lowered the barrel as he studied Ayden.

"Boston. It's a city in the State of Massachus—"

"I know where Boston is." The man with the torch gripped his arm. "You can explain to the captain."

The guard with the rifle took the reins from the ground and followed.

Ayden's hair, grown long and streaked with gray over the years, had come unbound from his topknot during the race to escape Rakesh. Dressed in a hip-length collarless kurta and worn work pyjamas, with his skin tanned dark, he appeared more native than Bostonian. When searched, they'd find similar clothing in the pack along with the Arabian robe. The only thing of value he carried was the amulet—a red stone on a worn metal chain.

They'll not know its value even without mind-magic.

He'd watched Rakesh wield subtle *earth-based mind-magic* for many years. The Indian magi used a type of sorcery his family would never have considered possible. Although confident he could imitate his former master, if necessary, he had never attempted the use of that intrusive *mind-magic* but would if it helped him get home.

Home.

He never thought to return to Boston—never imagined the magical enslavement had an end. Rakesh made him believe his service would be for life, and Ayden found no reason to think otherwise.

Until the coven-moon rose tonight.

He glanced up at the glowing orb as the guards escorted him into camp.

Eight tents faced a central campfire. The largest boasted a commander's badge beside the closed flap.

"The horse needs care," the soldier holding the gray's reins told his watch partner.

The man who gripped Ayden's arm nodded. "See to it. I'll speak with the captain."

They waited in silence near the fire until the flap over the large tent opened, and three men ducked through the passage.

"With the full moon to light our path, we can leave right away." A turbaned cavalry officer indicated the golden globe in the sky then straightened his uniform.

"Good. That will see you well on your way to the gulf by morning." The captain's gaze caught Ayden's, and he held up a hand of dismissal to the cavalry officer. "Who is this, private?"

"We found him near the camp perimeter. He claims to be American."

"I *am* American." Ayden straightened his shoulders and stared at the officer. "I seek aid to return home."

The commander stepped close and narrowed his eyes. "You don't look American."

"I've been in India for twenty years."

"He said he was a prisoner," the private added. "He wants asylum."

"Asylum?"

"Safety from the man who kept me prisoner, yes—but above all else, I wish to return home."

The officer studied Ayden for several moments and then tipped his head. "There's a cavalry unit leaving now. If you like, you may accompany them."

Ayden's chest relaxed as he exhaled. "I have a gelding—"

"His horse is being cared for by Private Syed," the guard said. "He had no saddle."

"Have Private Syed provision the horse. There are old saddles in the tack house."

"Yes, Sir." The private departed at a brisk pace.

"Thank you, sir. I was afraid you would deny my request."

"I would have except for one thing." The captain smiled. "I have a cousin who has lived in Boston most of his life. Two summers ago, we spent time together at our late grandmother's estate in London." He chuckled and grinned again at Ayden. "I teased him mercilessly over the way he spoke. I can hear him in your words. You are, indeed, an American." He gestured to the pot hanging above the fire. "If you're hungry, you should eat now."

Ayden took advantage of the offer, filling one of the stacked metal bowls with stew. "Where is the cavalry heading?"

"The Gulf of Cambay. You should be able to find a ship going around the horn, or better yet, an overland passage across Egypt to the Mediterranean."

"I have no money to purchase passage either way."

The commander shrugged as Private Syed returned with the gray. "I have a feeling you'll be able to manage. Find work on a merchant ship or in the harbor."

Ayden put his empty bowl with the others and offered the man his hand. "Again, you have my thanks. If you ever visit your cousin in Boston, be sure to look for Ayden MacKenna."

The captain took his hand. "I will, Mr. MacKenna. I wish you the best of luck."

Ayden mounted the gray, now fitted with a worn leather saddle.

Several riders passed the tents on their way down the trail on the far side of the camp.

The cavalry officer wearing the turban rode between the tents and reined in beside the commander. "A not so young recruit?" he asked as he watched Ayden mount.

"An American citizen under our protection, Lieutenant Wells. He wishes to return home."

Chapter 2

Ayden MacKenna

October 2, 1872 – North Atlantic near Boston harbor

The lookout called the sight of land as Ayden came on deck; his black robe flapped furiously in the wind. A steady breeze filled the sails and sent a fine ocean spray over the rail to cool Ayden's face and hands. He'd cut his hair and trimmed his beard, even purchased trousers and a frock coat in London, but he'd kept the robe. And the amulet.

"We've made good time this trip." Captain Meadows stopped at the rail beside Ayden.

"What do they say? Fair winds?"

"Aye, and following seas. This voyage has been all of that, especially for this time of year." The captain puffed his pipe and returned to his duties. He paused and remarked over his shoulder, "Highly unusual. A blessing indeed."

Ayden nodded and looked up at the full sails.

My fair wind. My following sea. You're welcome, Captain.

Hours spent watching the watery horizon had darkened Ayden's already tanned face and hands. Although, at times, it seemed his skin had permanently browned from the many years in the Indian desert.

Ahead, the glittering midday sun sparkled across the water, and he squinted at the harbor in the distance.

Almost home.

He'd scarce allowed himself to dream of this. Over twenty years had passed since he'd last seen this harbor. Cudgeled by the two cowardly James brothers, he'd been thrown into the hold of a foreign ship and right into the clutches of Magi Rakesh.

The journey from the British camp in the Aravalli Mountains had been a long one. Longer than he had anticipated.

The cavalry unit he traveled with made good time to the Gulf of Cambay. In the city of Surat, near the mouth of the Tapti River, he and the British had parted ways. The merchant vessels belonging to the British India Company were happy to take their brethren aboard. Not so with a penniless American.

He slept in alleyways and worked odd jobs, saving what little he earned. After a year, he was fortunate to find a working berth in the galley on a passenger vessel bound for Cyprus via the newly opened Suez Canal. From there, he worked his way as a galley man across the Mediterranean Sea to Algiers, then through the straits of Gibraltar to Lisbon. After that, he traveled by merchant's vessel to Portsmouth, England.

In Portsmouth, he worked as a bartender near the harbor. It was there he met Captain Meadows and negotiated a passenger's berth on Meadow's ship, scheduled to set sail for Boston within the next fortnight.

Another shout from the crow's nest drew him from his reverie, and he pushed the hood from his head and stared at the harbor as it drew nearer.

Many times, during his captivity, he'd tried to read his lover's fate in a fire. But visions of her ceased the day her brothers had trundled him like a pig and sold him to the dark-skinned magi.

Perhaps his vision couldn't span the ocean.

She'll be gone. Even if she remains in Boston, she'll have made a new life without me.

A woman as beautiful and talented as Margaret James would have had no difficulty finding another to replace him. He couldn't return with false hope, set on revenge, and expect to make a life for himself. Besides, there were other people he needed to find.

Like my parents and baby brother, Melvyn.

Whatever these years had bestowed upon the James brothers and his lovely Margaret, they would have to wait. He needed to find his family.

Gods, give me the strength to bind the vicious wound within my soul and leave it be.

As the ship sailed into the harbor, Ayden withdrew to the small cabin he shared with three other men. He removed and folded away his comfortable robes and pyjamas and dressed in the only western clothes he owned, a simple pair of slacks, a collarless cotton shirt, and a brown frock coat. He packed his few remaining items into his used carpetbag, tucked the amulet into his shirt, and returned to the deck.

Once the ship was tied off and the gangway secured, a port official came aboard to speak with the captain. He held the vessel's manifest while one of the young cabin boys brought a small writing desk and chair. After he seated himself at the top of the gangway, he began to process the passengers.

The port official glanced up from his record book. "Your name and place of birth, sir."

"Ayden MacKenna, born in New Haven, Connecticut. Returning home to Massachusetts."

"Welcome home, Mr. MacKenna. Next."

With a flick of his wrist, the official placed a check beside Ayden's name, and the pyromancer proceeded down the gangway to shore.

There were several things Ayden needed to do, too many for the time left in the day.

The pier seemed to rock beneath his feet as he dodged through sailors and merchants, holding tight to his bag.

A busy drinking establishment caught his eye. Revere's Tavern looked like an ideal place to seek employment if the patronage gave any indication. Surely, they needed someone who could pour a drink or sweep the floor.

He stepped inside and paused beside the entrance to allow his eyes to adjust to the shaded interior. A sparkling chandelier from a high ceiling filled the room with a dim but steady light. Men relaxed at the tables, some enjoying a meal and a few drinking and gambling.

The decorative rail from the staircase extended across the second-floor balcony above the bar. Women in various stages of undress lounged there, peering down onto the tavern floor. A thin redhead wiggled her fingers at him.

Ayden lowered his chin and made his way to the bar.

"What'll you have?" the white-shirted bartender asked as he wiped the counter with a towel.

"I'm looking for work." Ayden pointed to the dusty floor and several empty tables covered with dirty dishes. "I could keep this place tidy, the floor swept, and the tables clean."

The barkeep, shorter than Ayden, with a shiny bald pate and a thick handlebar mustache, narrowed his eyes and considered him. "I have a girl who cleans up." He scanned the bar, then shook his head and tossed the bar rag under the counter. "No telling where she's gotten off to—or with whom."

"I could start now."

The older gentleman considered Ayden's carpetbag, then tipped his head as if considering him. "You're no youngster. By the look of you, I'd say you've seen forty years or better. Just off a ship?"

"Yes, to both." Ayden set his bag down and leaned his elbows against the bar. "Boston is home—or was." He took a breath and smiled. "I've been away."

"And now you're back hoping for a fresh start."

"You're very perceptive."

"I've been tending bar a long time. You get that way." He lifted the hinged counter, stepped from behind the bar, and nodded to a younger man serving drinks from behind the counter. "My son," he said by way of explanation and extended his arm. "Let's talk." He pointed to an empty table and chair beside the bar then held out his hand. "Marion Tull."

Ayden took his hand in a firm grip. "Ayden MacKenna."

Marion took a seat as Ayden pushed his bag out of the way and sat across from him.

The bald man considered Ayden for several moments before he spoke. "It's not easy to start over." He raised his hand to forestall Ayden's comment. "And I do need someone trustworthy, older than my boy, who can take orders when we're busy, clean tables, and sweep up when we're slow."

"I can do all that. *Trust me.*" Desperate to land this opportunity, Ayden shaded his words with *earth-skill* like he'd observed Rakesh use for so many years.

"Do you have a place to stay?"

"Not yet."

You're fortunate to have met me.

Ayden placed the mental suggestion with *mind-magic* and promised himself Marion Tull would never regret this decision.

Marion ran a hand over his hairless head and watched two men enter the establishment. "I happen to have a room in the back. It used to be an office before I bought the upper floors from the landlord." He raised a bushy eyebrow at Ayden. "After you clean it out, you are welcome to stay there until you find something better."

Ayden smiled. "When do I start?"

"Clean out the room first, then come see me for the outside key. Take today and get your bearings. Have a bath and get cleaned up. You'll start tomorrow. We open at noon."

Their chairs scraped across the wooden floor as they came to their feet.

"Follow me, and I'll show you the room. Then I need to get back to work." Marion entered the back room and wound his way through stacked liquor crates, grain bags, and canned goods. "The kitchen is over there." He waved at the far side of the room. "You can find a meal there when you need one. Introduce yourself to Qiang first. Let him know you're a new hire."

Marion opened a wooden door and stepped back.

The ten by twelve rectangular room had a door and a dirty window that looked onto an alleyway. Empty pallets covered the floor.

"I appreciate the work and the room. I won't let you down." Ayden set his bag inside the dusty room and then shook Marion's hand again.

"It is my good fortune to have met you." Marion nodded as he stepped back. "Stack those pallets over there." He pointed to an empty corner of the stock room. "I need to get back to the bar. My young Harry can get overwhelmed when he's by himself. I'll have the key to that outside door when you're done."

Ayden watched his new employer hurry through the back room, then walked to the window and wiped a portion clean with the edge of an empty potato sack.

A coal stove stood in one corner, along with an empty coal bin.

It's not much, but it's a start.

Ayden had a lot to do before noon tomorrow. He needed a new suit of clothes or two. One set, appropriate for work, like the wool slacks and white cotton shirts Marion wore, the other town clothes, a winter jacket, and a hat. He lifted a corner of the nearest pallet and pulled it through the door into the stockroom.

He'd also find a bathhouse, a barber, and a used furniture dealer. After he accomplished what he needed to do today, he'd settle back in his new room and build a small fire.

He needed to stare into the flames and find out what he could see.

The Soul of the Witch Saga continues in Book 2:

Pyromancer

Also by

Soul of the Witch Saga

Prodigy – Book 1

Pyromancer – Book 2

Passage – Book 3

Prophecy – Book 4

Paradox – Book 5

Patriarch – Book 6

—

J.L.'s Timeless Quest

Aubrielle's Call

The Corsair's Tempest

Hawthorn and Mistletoe

—

The Hunter Chronicles

Hunter's Gamble

Hunter and Lily Graham

The Kid in Black

Penelope's Heart

All of these stories take place within the same shared universe.

About the Author

C. (Connie) Marie Bowen writes paranormal romance and historical fantasy set within a richly layered, persistent universe. Her award-winning novel *Passage* launched the *Soul of the Witch* series, introducing a world where magic, loyalty, and sacrifice intertwine.

Bowen's stories span multiple series, with characters crossing paths and timelines within the shared universe of the Soul of the Witch Saga. Figures such as Hunter from *The Hunter Chronicles* and J.L. from *The Timeless Quest* play meaningful roles within this interconnected world.

Born in Denver, Colorado, Bowen grew up with a love of ghost stories and storytelling. She now lives in the greater Chicagoland area with her husband and two rescue pets, Abigail and Rousseaux.

Visit https://www.cmariebowen.com to explore her connected series and learn more.